A LAST HOPE

VERITY SANDAHL

DEDICATION

To my children.

God chose you before the foundation of the world.

May you always find your hope in Him, the perfect Author.

"For this reason I bow my knees before the Father... that according to the riches of his glory he may grant you to be strengthened with power through his Spirit in your inner being, so that Christ may dwell in your hearts through faith—that you, being rooted and grounded in love, may have strength to comprehend with all the saints what is the breadth and length and height and depth, and to know the love of Christ that surpasses knowledge, that you may be filled with all the fullness of God. — Ephesians 3:14-19

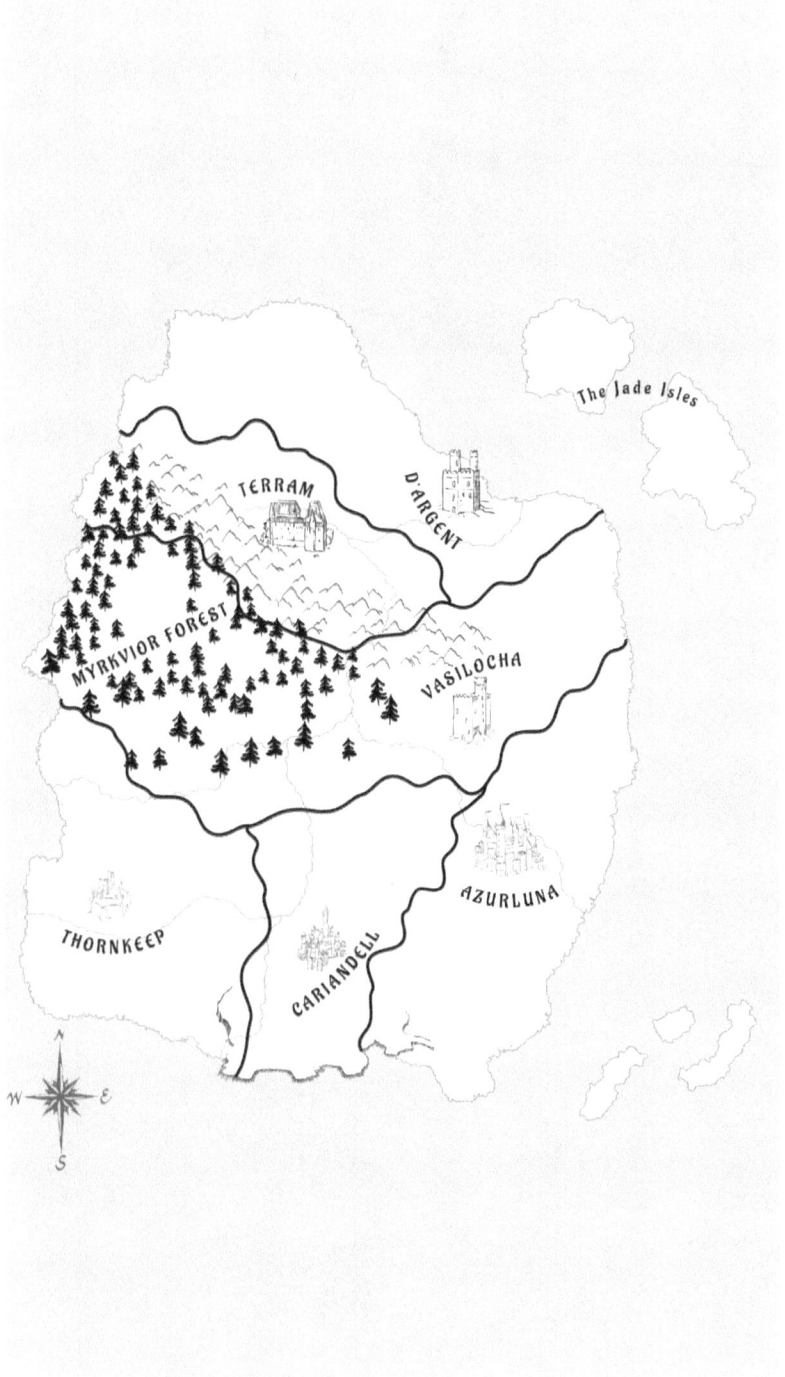

The Jade Isles

TERRAM

D'ARGENT

MYRKVIOR FOREST

VASILOCHA

THORNKEEP

CARIANDELL

AZURLUNA

N
W · E
S

CHAPTER 1

ONCE EVERY THOUSAND YEARS, TWO SOULS ARE ENTWINED, UNITING THE POWERS OF THE KINGDOMS.

*M*ountains of treats, magic tricks, and more silver and gold than eight-year-old Prince Marc had known existed.

The week had been magical.

Now, sitting in a garden larger than the town Marc had grown up in, he tipped his head back, looking up at the night sky. It sparkled with a thousand white stars – just like the shimmering silk and diamond-studded flags that adorned every window of their hosts' palace.

"All that silk," Uncle Amis had said. "What a waste."

"King Thrush has the money to buy silk, and anything else he pleases." Marc's father had grumbled.

Marc knew his father must be telling the truth,

for never had he seen so much food or splendor. Even the palace floors were not the rough limestone of his castle at home but rather a reflective, glass-like stone that his father called marble.

But his favorite part of all was his new friend, Princess Arianna.

Of course, his twin brother, Thomis, teased that Marc liked her, but Arianna was just interesting.

She laughed at his jokes and teased him back. She was much more exciting than any girl he'd ever met, and tonight, she was going to show him how she could fly!

He'd heard all the people in Arianna's noble family could fly, but he'd never actually seen it. Marc's family had magical powers as well, but his father made him keep his powers a secret though he couldn't understand why. They were not nearly as splendid as Arianna's!

He pulled impatiently at the ruby pin his father had insisted he wear on his collar "to show his position," and swung his feet back and forth as he listened for Arianna.

Finally, a child's footsteps pummeled down the gravel path, and Marc stood to see his friend.

Even though she was also eight years old, she was almost a head shorter than he, but despite her tiny size, she had the biggest, most joyful laugh that filled the whole garden when she saw him.

She ran forward, her black hair shooting behind her as if she were one of the stars on the flags. So magical – and so high above him.

But wasn't she? Arianna was the future queen of this magical place.

While he was a future king, his own little castle seemed like a toy compared to hers, and his abilities, the ones his father said not to tell others about, were so unexciting when held to flying.

He smiled. "So, you can really fly?"

She nodded, and her luminescent golden brown eyes sparkled as her feet slowly lifted from the gravel walk, hovering a few feet above the ground. "It's not flying as much as climbing the air around me." She giggled, reaching out and touching a branch above his head, "I hold on to the air, just like I can hold on to this branch – or your hand."

Swooping down, she grabbed his hand, but as her small fingers closed around his, everything changed.

In a flash, Marc felt a rushing around him, and he was thrust upward.

Terror pulsed through him as his own feet shot up from the ground. He could feel the air. It pushed around him, forcing him higher and higher.

He struggled against it, but it only shoved him up faster.

Arianna shrieked as they bolted not a few feet, but a hundred feet into the sky as if their joint fear drove them both farther than they meant.

"Put us down!" he begged, flailing far above the top of the donjon, but keeping hold of her hand for fear of losing the one solid thing he had.

She flailed beside him. "I – I have to push the air past me, but it's fighting me."

Her massive eyes rounded in the moonlight. "Marc, *you* are pushing the air!"

Anger jolted between them, adding heat to Marc's terror.

That was impossible.

"I can't fly! I can't do that. That's what *you* can do."

But she was adamant. "You have to push the air above your head, or we will not get down."

"I – can't." He pushed his free hand out to show her, but as he did, he felt the air push against his palm.

He could control the air. She was right. He was doing it.

Frantically, he drew his palm above his head, pushing at the air. It felt like pillows against his palm, but if he pressed carefully, he could control it.

His anger subsiding, he pressed again and lowered several feet.

"Together!" Arianna commanded.

Desperate to lower, Marc watched her small hand pushing around her, syncing his movements with her.

Was she using her feet? Yes, she walked down the air like stairs.

He tried to climb down with his feet, finding with shock he could do the same.

And suddenly, they were descending together, smoothly and perfectly in unison.

But the moment Marc's feet hit the ground, he jumped away from her, letting the anger return.

"You didn't warn me!" he bellowed.

"I – I didn't know!"

"How did you do that?

"I've never done that to anyone before. I've heard it in the old stories that sometimes people can fly with us, but I didn't think it could really happen!"

Was she lying? He could tell, but then he'd have to touch her again.

He reached for her hand.

"Promise you won't make me fly," he demanded.

She laughed. "You don't want to touch me."

"Promise!" He kept his hand outstretched.

She frowned. "I promise."

She stood still, blinking at him, and Marc swallowed. He was afraid to touch her, but he knew that he was supposed to be brave. Wasn't he a future king?

He couldn't be afraid of a girl! Even a pretty one that could apparently drop him from a great distance should she choose —

Closing his eyes, he concentrated hard.

Like the royal bloodline of her land, his royal line also had a special power, though he thought it was far less exciting. All of his family line except for Marc's twin brother, Thomis, could feel people's feelings through touch.

His hand shook a little as he reached out, touching her arm.

Marc was still learning his power, but he had found each emotion felt different, and it was easy to recognize that Arianna was worried.

Worry was like fear but steadier, like a dull aching in your head.

He tried to think what he wanted to ask. "Did you know it would do that? Did you know you could force me to fly?"

"No!"

Marc waited. He'd learned that when someone lied, their heart flipped, and then their feelings struggled, twisting between the lightening of hope that their lie would be believed and the darkness of guilt.

No twisting, just a warm pressing of her earnestness. She spoke truth.

Yet something was rising within her – a new fear

that overshadowed the terror he'd felt even as he floated above the castle peaks.

"Why are you upset?" he demanded.

"I – I think it could be terrible!" she gasped. "To fly with someone who is not of our line is rare – so much so that my nurse says it may happen to one of us in a lifetime or even every hundred years."

"Then this magic must be very special!" He opened his eyes.

Arianna was shaking her head, her dark hair waving around her face in the darkness. "It's serious, Marc. I think our souls are connected now."

Marc didn't think it sounded bad at all. He could fly as long as he was with her, and he liked her. Maybe Father would let him visit again next summer – and the next.

He looked over at her and noticed that he'd ripped her sleeve when he'd grabbed her arm. "Here. I'll fix that."

He pulled off the small ruby pin he'd been wearing. It would look just right holding up her silky sleeve.

She blinked down at the pin as he tried to pin it on. "I didn't mean to, but we will always be."

"Be what?" He was concentrating hard. For some reason, it seemed like accidentally poking her with the pin would be the worst thing in the world.

Strange, he'd never cared much about not hurting anyone before.

Her eyes were huge. "Connected. Souls don't disconnect."

He laughed. "That's good. I'd not want my soul ripped."

He stepped back to study his handiwork. The pin was crooked, but it was holding her silky sleeve up so he decided he had done a good job.

She was frowning as she lifted her luminescent golden brown eyes to him.

Luminescent.

How was that even possible?

Weren't brown eyes dark and deep? And yet these were almost star-like, full of emotion and changing color as the torchlight reflected in them.

Amidst the brown were green, gold, and specks of darker browns.

Marc had never been very aware of girls - until this moment.

And now, he felt his tongue grow thick.

But then she gave him a shy smile. "Would you like to fly again?"

"Yes, please!" He grabbed her hand, and he felt she was only happy, and they lifted slightly.

This time, he didn't panic, letting the air carry him

up. As long as he was holding her hand, he could push the air around him, and he loved it. In a few minutes he was spinning her with him and pushing faster and faster.

"Can we go higher?" he asked.

As high as before? She teased.

He felt her thrill, and he laughed. "As high as you want, Princess Arianna."

They rose to the tops of the garden wall and then higher. This time, Marc was not afraid.

Their joy combined, and they climbed the air, bringing it into subjection under their feet, swimming through it, each with one hand while holding tight to each other.

"We could spin through that arch and then fly up past the top of that tree," he offered.

"There is a fountain on the other side." She motioned, her skirt floating around her. "We could soar down from the tree then and touch it."

Without another word they soared up, shooting toward the arch, spinning easily and then catapulting toward the tree. Marc's fingers scraped across the bristly branches.

He wanted to hit the tree again, and somehow Arianna knew that. They rose again, zipping around the tree and then another and another before soaring several feet above the garden path.

The wind, wild and listless, blew around him, and he reached out, bending it and grabbing a fistful of it.

Then they doubled back toward the arch, no longer needing to speak. They both flew as one, somehow knowing what the other wanted.

Marc knew he'd never experienced such magic. This was something special.

Maybe it was only for children or best friends.

Maybe it had something to do with the soul connection Arianna had cried about. Why would she cry about such a thing? It was wonderful!

"Marc! Prince Marc!" a man's voice bellowed into the darkness, and the two children froze in midair before hurriedly, lowering to the gravel.

"Swear you'll not tell!" she whispered, her hand still in his.

He felt the tremor of fear and squeezed her hand. "I'll keep the secret - always." he promised. A strange urge to protect her secret — and her — whelmed up and warmed him until he was sure he'd burst.

The footsteps that belonged to the voice were marching toward them, and Marc only had a second to catch her relieved smile in the darkness before Uncle Amis swung around the corner and strode quickly up to them.

His uncle's face was strangely white in the moonlight. "I've been looking for nigh unto half an hour,

Marc. Your father commands you to come with me at once."

Marc's uncle was a tall, thin man who rarely showed emotion, but now he grabbed Marc's arm with a surprisingly tight grip.

"We'll both come." Marc straightened his frame, which was half of Uncle Amis' size.

"He called for only you. Leave the princess."

It was not Uncle Amis' place to speak to Marc in such a way! Marc was the future king.

He held her hand tighter, unsure why he felt the need to.

He'd never had a little sister, but now he felt like an older brother. He could not leave her in a dark garden.

"I'll walk Princess Arianna inside." he offered, awkwardly fumbling through the new feeling of concern for someone else. Where had this come from?

"I'll wait for you here." She smiled, slipping her hand out of his.

"I won't be long."

Uncle Amis was pulling his arm. "You must obey your father, now."

Marc resisted the urge of instant obedience, turning to look at Princess Arianna."I'll come back for you," he promised.

It was a silly promise, but whether it was the

grumpiness in Uncle Amis or the magic of the night, Marc needed to make it. He was only eight, but he knew he shouldn't leave her. Of course, it was silly. There was no danger. There was no reason for the promise, but he meant it with all his soul.

And then Uncle Amis pushed him around the corner, and she was gone from his sight.

Now, he could feel Uncle Amis' feelings as his uncle pushed him. His uncle was anxious, and every so often he could feel his uncle's heart spike with fear.

Father must be very angry that I slipped off, Marc thought.

He didn't care. Even if his father spanked him, he wouldn't care. He'd flown! And he'd made a best friend, and for some odd reason, that was just as exciting.

He wished he could fly to his father. It would save so much time!

And what would his father say if he saw Marc flying?

No, it's a secret. I'll never tell a soul, not even Thomis. He reminded himself.

The sadness of not getting to share lasted only seconds. He shared it with Arianna, his best friend.

Oh! He hoped father would be quick so he could run back to her!

He glanced around. The garden was gigantic, ten

times the size his garden at home, and he'd not thought about where they were going.

They were now far from the palace. They'd walked the opposite way, and here there were no torches, leaving them to curve through dark mazes of bushes and statues.

"Father is here?" Marc demanded.

"Up here," his uncle said, but his uncle's heart skipped, and then the older man heated.

"He's not," Marc countered.

"He wants you to come up here, Marc," Uncle Amis admitted.

Marc checked. Uncle Amis' heart beat fast, but his words were true.

And then they came to a gate at the back of the garden, and just outside it were several horses.

Even in the dark, Marc recognized some of his father's most trusted knights.

Uncle Amis pushed him through the gate. "There is an attack tonight, Marc."

Attack? Marc didn't understand. Yet, he realized one thing: Arianna was back there where the attack would occur.

"Arianna!" He yelled.

He had to warn her! She really was in danger.

He tried to twist out of his uncle's grip, his feet scrambling out from under him as his uncle held fast.

"It's for your safety, nephew."

"I have to get her!" Gravel kicked up around them as Marc struggled desperately.

"You must go, my prince!"

"I – promised!"

His uncle was a thin, academic man, but he was full grown, and Marc was only eight.

Still, Marc would not give up. He fought blindly. He'd promised his friend, and he had to get her.

But more hands were coming to help his uncle. His father's knights were grabbing him, and despite all his efforts, they were dragging him through the gate.

Marc gripped the iron that protruded from the thick stone wall. "I promised her!" he yelled.

Uncle Amis jerked Marc up hard, tearing Marc's sweaty palms from the iron gate.

"No!" Marc lunged back through the gate.

"Please!" He shouted, and while it was a yell, it was also a prayer. Arianna was in danger, and he needed the One Father to hear him and protect her until Marc could get back to her.

Pelting forward, he made it several yards from the gate, but one of the knights had caught up to him and lunged, knocking Marc to the ground.

Marc's head hit the gravel, and everything went black.

The cool night settled around Arianna as she sat quietly on the stone bench. Her father had said that Terram was a rough and superstitious country, but Prince Marc was kind and gentlemanly. Maybe the soul bond – even to a boy from Terram - was not a bad thing. How could something so wonderful be bad?

How had she done it? She wasn't sure, but she hoped it would be alright.

Her mother had died birthing Arianna, and while she spent her life surrounded by servants, she had never had a friend. Perhaps, a soul bond may be a nice thing considering how lonely she often was. Maybe it was alright in certain situations.

A scream split the night air, and Arianna jumped to her feet.

More screams and shouts started from the palace, and instinctively she stepped back into the darkness.

Something terrible was happening within.

A few guards came out to the garden, shooting up into the night air, and Arianna was relieved to see a large and powerful knight fly up into the air with two other nobles, but as they reached the top of the walls, large, dark webs shot out from the towers, and in seconds all three men were flailing, caught fast by the ropes.

"They're on the walls!" came a shout, and Arianna stepped back, crouching deep into the hedge. She could barely feel the sharp twigs scratching her face and arms as she curled into a ball, praying they'd not find her.

But they were trying.

In seconds, strange soldiers were everywhere, their boots making the garden shake.

She curled in further, trembling as the nightmare erupted everywhere around her. She watched for her father's guards, but none came. The soldiers were of Terram.

She closed her eyes, tightening further. The screams and shouts ran together, but then, a new sound added to the din. It was a strange crackling, and the blackness around her was turning orange, and her nostrils were starting with the sharp odor of smoke.

Fire!

In seconds the cool night air was warming, and Arianna rolled out from under her bush, tumbling into the gravel walk to see tendrils of flame break down the garden vines and engulf the summer-dried trees.

Where could she escape? She turned toward the castle, but several windows already glowed with flame.

She'd have to go deeper into the garden, but she knew the enemy soldiers were there.

Shaking, she shot into another hedge, hoping to stay ahead of the flames, but they were growing fast.

"My lady!"

Arianna blinked into the darkness. Who?

A woman dressed as a lady in waiting stood there. She was slender and graceful. Despite the screams around the palace, she stood in absolute calm, and somehow, she was looking right through the darkness and into the hedge where Arianna crouched.

"This way, my lady. Hurry!"

"Did - my father send you?" Arianna asked, knowing

"Nay, princess, but I am sent to protect and help you by One greater than your father."

Arianna hesitated. No one was greater than her father.

"What is your name?" She glanced behind the lady at the growing flames.

"Laelynn. Now, you must come with me."

The lady appeared so kind - and so calm despite the fire which now surrounded them on three sides that Arianna realized she had no choice but to trust the lady.

"This way!" The lady pushed her forward.

Arianna could hear the soldiers, but somehow, the lady evaded them, always managing to stay on a different side of the wall than their enemies.

Finally, they rounded the last bend, and Arianna gasped in relief.

Aethelgard, her beloved old maid stood there.

The old woman reached for her and Arianna raced into her embrace, but then she looked around and realized where they were. While they were against an outer wall, they were trapped in a dead end in the maze of garden walk-ways.

She blinked into the black night, trying to think of a place to hide, but the shrubs were low here.

She looked desperately at the lady who was handing a large bag to Aethelgard.

"For your travels," she murmured.

"But we cannot escape from here." Arianna squeaked. "We are trapped!"

The mysterious lady's voice was gentle. "Fear not my lady. It is the will of a higher Power that you live tonight." The lady's voice was absolute, and as she spoke, she reached for the stone wall.

The stones fell always as if they were fabric, and Arianna stared.

Had there been a passage?

The lady motioned them through the wall, and Arianna and her nurse jumped through.

Then the wall closed behind them, and they were alone, racing to the black forest.

But at the edge of the wood, Arianna paused under its shadow and looked back at her home. The screams had long since stopped, and from this distance, she could not hear the soldiers running. From here, her beautiful home looked like a big flaming grave, rising ominously against the star-lit sky.

And wasn't it a grave?

Something burning and cold settled in her soul.

Her father was dead. She knew it unquestioningly. The indestructible giant had been slain, and her people were defeated in a single hour of betrayal.

But more had died than that — more than her people and her line.

Something in her had died too.

Hope. All hope was gone.

The lady read her thoughts. "No, child. There is a last hope."

Numbly, Arianna turned to look into the kind face.

The lady touched Arianna's temple. "This will

help protect you. The Simmins nobility can feel people's feelings. This is a protection spell that will keep them from reading yours."

Deep inside, Arianna felt a small wall go up. The lady had put something inside her! But Arianna was more stunned by the truth the lady had shared.

Marc had used his powers on her. That was why he'd wanted to touch her hands when he thought she was lying.

He'd betrayed her too. He'd lied to her, letting her think he had no powers.

Marc's betrayal was the worst of all.

The lady was wrong. There was no last hope.

It had been five weeks since she'd lost everything, and Arianna could not remember what it felt like to not be hungry.

She could hear Aethelgard's coughing from across the dark docks and shivered, the sharp sea air seeping through her already damp clothes. She stared into a small fire. It was one of several that dotted the camp along with wagons and circles of huddled people all hoping for passage on the last of three ships pulling out this night.

A boy her age stood at the next fire over speaking to a man. The boy's handsome young face was turned toward her, but he was looking at the man whose back was to Arianna.

As she watched, the boy stretched out a trembling hand palm-down over a small bucket of water at his feet.

The water flickered up, quadrupling in size, but then in an instant, it was quietly back in the bucket.

Arianna blinked. What had she just seen?

The boy raised his gaze and saw her.

He strode over to her, his face tight. "You saw me put *dirt* in that pot?"

"I - yes." Arianna replied knowing dirt would not have caused the water to raise as it had.

The boy shifted, studying her several seconds before deciding she was not a threat. "I can do magic tricks with - dirt - and the like." He gave an exaggerated shrug. "It's easy tricks, you know."

"It looks like good tricks," she agreed.

"It is." The boy continued to look at her. He had a sharply carved face for a child, and his eyes were dark grey and turbulent.

He spoke again, calm enough to try to hide the same coastal accent that Arianna herself was hiding, training his tongue not to curl around the consonants but to spit them out as the people of Terram did.

"I'm Casimir. I'm going to travel with the gypsies and do those kind of tricks – with dirt and water and such. What can you do?"

Arianna shivered in the warm dark cloak Laelynn had given her. What could she do?

Aethelgard had thought she could dance. Arianna had always loved to dance, but now she felt her tongue stick to her mouth.

How could she possibly dance? What if someone recognized her? What if she made a mistake and was thrown out?

She guessed why Aethelgard had brough her here. The old woman's health was waning, and likely, Aethelgard had very little time left.

Arianna looked up at the boy named Casimir, and shook her head slowly.

"I don't know," she whispered, beginning to tremble. Cold and mud had become a part of her the previous weeks. She wasn't sure they'd ever wash off, or if she could remember what it felt like to not have numb feet and hands.

Aethelgard had had a good plan, but even the best plans do not work when enough stacks against them.

The rain had started in the middle of the first

night, soaking through the common clothes that had been in the pack and seeping into their skin.

Arianna hated it, but it had been worse for Aethelgard, and Arianna knew the old woman was leaving her here because Aethelgard didn't have much longer to live.

And if the gypsies didn't agree to her staying, she'd have nowhere to go.

She turned and walked farther from the boy, trying to draw a deep breath, but she was too afraid.

Where was she to go? How would she survive?

"You can stop that fear from hurting you."

Arianna swung around. Somehow, the man who'd been talking to the boy had spanned the distance and come to stand behind her. It happened so quickly that she'd not seen it though he could not have moved fast; he was so relaxed.

He was leaning against a tree, his movements un-menacing yet there was something different – magical even – that made him look not quite — human.

It reminded her of the mysterious lady though the man was in every way her opposite. The lady had been so tender in her movements, and this man seemed so...quick and calculated.

He was smiling, the slight glow of the nearest fire making his white teeth gleam, but Arianna took a small step back.

Surely in the dark, she was imagining things. This was just a man.

"I – am not afraid." She whispered.

"Yes. You are. But you don't have to be. You just need to take that spell that's inside you and be smarter with how you use it."

He laughed when she started. He knew?

He knew about the spell that the lady had put inside her?

He gave a cold chuckle. "Yes. It's like a little wall that my dear old cousin tucked away in you, and like any wall, you can put things – like all your fear - behind it. So, you see, my dear. You don't need to be afraid. You can be strong."

Could it be true? Oh, to be rid of the fear that had made her sick for weeks! Arianna closed her eyes.

There was so much to be afraid of, so much evil had been done to her, and it made her tremble from the top of her head to the ends of her toes.

She felt it all, and she hated it. He was right to say it made her weak. Carefully, starting with the tips of her fingers, she started to catch all the fear and pull it to herself until it was in a small, blazing ball, held inside her mind, and then with one great force of will, she pushed it over the wall –

And it was gone!

Arianna opened her eyes. She felt nothing except the cold night. She was untouchable!

They'd taken her kingdom and her father, but they'd not be able to touch her now!

She looked around to thank the man, but he'd disappeared, and it was only Aethelgard coming back with a big gypsy.

He was businesslike and cold though his face did not show cruelty.

"What is her name?" he asked.

"Aria-" Aethelgard stopped herself in time when the damage was only partly done. A completely different name would have been safer, but a partial change would have to do.

"Aria?" The gypsy repeated. "Is she healthy? We don't need no sickness brought to Vacilocha. I have fifty people who want passage with us, and I have room for only one. She needs to be able to bring something to our performance, and this child is far too young to be able to do much of anything."

He started to turn away, but Arianna would not be abandoned again. Grabbing his arm, she forced him to pause.

Aethelgard was trying not to cough, but she choked out desperately. "The girl is healthy, and she can dance."

The gypsy looked down at Arianna, clearly unconvinced. "How well?"

No fear stopped Arianna as she stared up at him. "I can dance so well, you'll think I'm flying."

CHAPTER 2

THE CASTLE IN TERRAM: 13 YEARS LATER

*N*o king should be forced to marry against his will. What was the use of being king if you were subject to ridiculous laws and foolish rules?

King Marc Simmins shook Burgess Tinman's hand, holding it an extra second to make sure he read the man correctly.

Aye, he had.

Burgess Tinman's frustration had evaporated. Telling him that his daughter was pretty had done much to cool the council member's temper.

In truth, Marc could not remember what the girl looked like. The dreamy-eyed village girls all looked alike, following him around like he was the prize pig at the fair.

Everyone knew that Marc had to marry.

According to law, today should be his wedding day, for it was his 21st birthday, but a few compliments in just the right places, a small gift or two to the right people, and he'd convinced the council members that the age-old law was archaic.

"You are right, my king. We want a queen that is as noble as you, sire."

No flipping in the man's chest. He spoke truth.

Marc clapped him on the back. "To be sure, I will find a queen soon, Thad."

He felt the man warm at the personal title, and Marc added, "We have worked together for peace, and I mean to preserve it for the next generation."

The man nodded vigorously, and Marc had his footman usher him out, letting himself breathe out a sigh of relief only when alone.

That was the last council member to assure the issue would not be pushed.

But truly, who would question the foolish old law? The people were just glad for the peace and prosperity that Marc's reign had finally brought.

It had taken all his ability, but in the two years he'd become king, he'd ended the war between the kingdoms.

It should never have gone as long as it had, but the people of the coast were a proud, strong people. Marc's father had expected them to bow quickly when he'd wiped out the D'argent nobility, the members of the Thrush family in one, terrible night, but the people of the D'argent Kingdom had refused.

His father had needed allies and discovered that King Thrush had made other enemies. It had been an easy choice to make a deal with the queen of the Jade Isles But when the coastal land of D'argent was weakened, pirates sent out by the king of the Jade Isles had attacked the vulnerable cities, leaving orphans aplenty and ravaging the once-strong kingdom.

But Marc had found a solution. He'd been working with the people of the Jade Isles to help them establish their trade routes and had also been building back the destroyed buildings in D'argent.

It was pricey, but the peace was holding, and at the coming autumn ball, he meant for a peace treaty to be signed with a magic that could not be revoked.

Soon, there would be permanent peace, and Marc had done it.

To ask for a marriage of love was a small token to ask in return.

Marc crossed to the massive window overlooking his personal garden and let out a long sigh of relief.

Once upon a time, Marc would have thought that both love and peace would be his through the thousand-year-old prophesy.

Once every thousand years, two souls are entwined, uniting the powers of the kingdoms.

How could that not have been prophesying about him and Arianna? How else would he have been able to fly with her?

But if the prophecy had been about them, it wasn't now. Arianna had died the night of the attack, and the kingdoms were left divided, not united.

But Marc had worked hard to attain the peace, and he'd done it!

And love? Maybe, that would just never be.

Marc frowned down at his beloved garden, his haven from the constant stress of duty, and realized he may never share it with anyone.

It was a dark thought on his twenty-first birthday, but he couldn't quite let it go.

"What is a gelada?" Marc's twin brother, Thomis' voice cut into Marc's thoughts.

Marc turned. His brother stood in the doorway, the thick ledger spread across his arms.

Marc sighed. It was their birthday. Why would Thomis think to look through the money ledger on their birthday?

"A beautiful creature native to the Jade Isles." Marc shrugged, a tint of guilt mixing with his mood. "The Ecoptian delegates from the Jade Isles told me it is native to their land and a perfect pet for a...king of my stature. How could I not buy myself a birthday present?"

"Along with the shipload of stone and silks you purchased from them?" Thomis glowered. "For years, they pirated our borders —"

"And I made peace with them."

"Aye. You have. Why should they commit piracy when they can steal from you by trade?"

Thomis tossed the book on to the mahogany desk. "You are catering to our enemies."

"I am showing them good faith, and as a result of my efforts, there has been no bloodshed in two years. I told their delegates we wanted to buy and sell with them, and while they seem to have much to sell, the peace is holding."

Thomis' nostrils flared. "If only this peace were as intact as your arrogance, brother."

"Mayhap, I have something to be arrogant about. All is well, and it will be even better. When we sign the peace treaty sealed with magic, we will finally secure the peace between the three kingdoms.

Thomis froze. "What kind of magic?"

Marc didn't want to tell him, and he tried to laugh to lighten the words. "Dragon's blood."

Thomis gaped. "Dragon's blood! Are you mad? Anyone who breaks a contract written in dragon's blood will have their lands consumed in fire!"

"And thus our enemies will no longer be able to attack us by piracy. They are signing the contract too."

Thomis' brows were down so far, his eyes almost disappeared. "Where did you get the dragon's blood?

Marc hated to admit this part. "Well, they had it."

Thomis snapped to attention. "And they suggested it, I assume? Are you sure they do not have more at play, brother?"

Marc laughed. "You are always thinking the worst of others,

"I am merely thinking of my opponent's potential advantages!" Thomis had started pacing.

Would Thomis ruin their birthday over this?

"You agreed the terms of the contract were good." Marc pointed out.

Thomis was frowning. "That is what I cannot figure out. They are too good. Why would they agree to it?"

"Too good?" Marc laughed. "Do you hear yourself. How can a contract be too good?" He tried a new approach. "Let us take a walk brother. The day is beautiful. The gardens are in full bloom, and you and I are twenty-one today!"

Thomis sighed turning toward the garden, the tension in his face showing he was not done. "But a gelada, Marc?"

Marc chuckled. "Imagine it in the garden, Thomis. I am sure it is a beautiful creature as lovely as its name. I've been told it can smile."

Arianna watched the line of merchants stopped on the drawbridge.

Hundreds of times the protection spell Laelynn had placed inside her had held. Today would be no different, but her mission was dangerous, and one misstep —

"Do you always stop and watch before entering?" a deep voice murmured from behind her.

Casimir!

"You should not be here!" Arianna ducked into the shadows of the wooded tree line to stand beside him.

"They are too busy preparing for the cocky king's birthday feast to notice an extra face."

Casimir's handsome mouth turned into a real smile, a rarity for him when he was not performing.

A thread of fear hit Arianna. Surely, he wasn't going to attempt to enter into the castle – he wouldn't dare.

She grabbed his arm. "You won't try?"

He sighed. "No, I am not going to cross into the castle with you. You know I will not get past the guard. I wish I could though."

It had been thirteen years since the two had met, and Casimir had grown in strength as much as she had grown in weakness.

He could flip over the heads of his audience and do magic tricks with water – all fantastic circus tricks, but also part of his preparing with the small rebel force that she knew he had slowly built as the gypsies traveled around the two kingdoms.

His health was a sharp contrast to Arianna's for she had broken her leg three years earlier and could only walk with a pronounced limp.

But one thing she could do – enter the castle. She glanced past him to the castle and then back, thankful that the protection spell allowed her to still help the rebel cause.

"Be careful, Aria." His voice tensed.

"You know I enter the castle often."

"But not -" He rubbed his hands together in frustration. "I hate this. I hate that you are the one -"

"I'm the only one." She raised her chin proudly.

He surprised her with a second smile. "Yes, you are, you stubborn girl!"

"Then let me go."

For several seconds he stood, but then he nodded. They both knew what needed to be done.

Arianna stepped toward the drawbridge which was unusually full.

Several men sat on horses, their clothing the pompously bright silks of the Jade Isles and their steeds as decked out as they were.

Two huge carts sat behind them laden with boxes and a large cage covered in a bright silk drape.

Arianna watched them coldly. Despite them being at the end of the drawbridge closest to the huge iron gate, the leader's loud voice rang through the morning air.

"It is unfit that we should be kept waiting. We are the ambassadors of Ecoptia."

His gaze swept back and landed on Arianna. "And it stinks back here."

The guard smiled. "All must come through this gate. 'Tis tradition."

The Ecoptian muttered something under his breath in his own language, and Casimir bristled, but she ignored the haughty ambassador.

One of the things she loved most about working at the tannery was that it caused her to smell and made the people the people of Terram stay away from her.

The guard did not seem to like the men either, his

mouth set in a faker-than-normal grin as he circled around them.

It felt good to know Casimir watched. She'd been through this gate two hundred times before, but today was different, and by the time she reached the bridge, her limp had worsened from trembling.

Still, she boldly met the guard's gaze as she paused second in line of the merchants lined up on the massive drawbridge waiting to enter through the white-washed castle wall.

She hoped that her whole frame did not shake from the beating of her heart! That would be the one thing that would give her away.

"Theo!" The guard stepped forward, all his teeth showing as he clapped the villager in front of her on the back.

Despite his girth which settled largely in the middle, the guard, a cousin of the arrogant king, did not frighten the other villagers on the bridge, each willingly extending his hand to shake the hefty man's hand or be drawn into a cheerful hug.

He almost didn't even look like a guard despite the sword strapped at his broad side.

Arianna knew better.

Like all the Simmins, he feigned friendliness, and this greeting he did, a false sign that there was only peace after a decade of war, was a test.

He had the power of the Simmins and his harmless greetings invaded their souls for unbeknownst to them, he was feeling their intentions, making sure none passed with ill-intent in their hearts.

She'd seen him stiffen when he saw her in his peripheral vision, and now he turned his fake grin on her.

"You are early today, Aria." He smiled at her over the head of the short man in front of her before turning his full attention to the man.

"Crispis, something disturbs you today." The guard said.

If she had not known what the guard was really doing, she'd have thought he cared, but of course he didn't. He felt something threatening, and he was making sure that there was nothing the man meant to do.

The short muscled villager, Crispis, was no threat of course.

The only threat to the Simmins entering the castle was Arianna, thin, halting woman that she be.

"Our two-year-old daughter is sick. I fear for her." The broad tailor, Crispis sighed.

Arianna saw the guard's face relax. "Petir, the best physician in the country, is visiting for the king's birthday. You will go to him. I served with him on the coast. He is probably now in the great hall, and you tell him I sent you. I've a mind that he'd help you for little to no cost. He loves children.

Then the wretch would not have been on the coast or participated in the war where so many children were orphaned. Arianna thought, plastering on her own smile and stepping toward the guard.

The guard made a show of shaking her hand as he did every Wednesday, his eyes darting as he tried to read her.

Most weeks, she'd enjoy his frustration.

Not today.

Little could get past her nervousness, but she'd promised Casimir she could do it.

Moments later, he waved her by, and she clumsily tripped through the gate and paused at the edge of the courtyard as she always did, scanning for the king though she knew that he would be in town today.

Marc Simmins, the one man who may recognize her from childhood went to town every Wednesday, and that was why she came to the castle on Wednesdays.

And she'd managed to avoid him for three years this way.

A few times, she'd run into his twin brother, Prince Thomis, and frozen in fear, afraid she'd be recognized, but seeing Marc from a distance had trained her to see that he and his identical twin were very different.

While their coloring and builds were similar, both fair with warm red-tinted blond hair and vibrant blue eyes, there it ended.

King Marc walked with an ease and a smile perpetually playing at his lips, his warm-gold hair tousled and shaking around his head in a way that would have fit a town-boy better than a king.

Conversely, Prince Thomis' gold hair was combed straight back, making the muscular features and ever-taught jaw stand out. His movements were calculating and tense, and the vibrant blue eyes that sparkled in his older twin brother were cold in him, untrusting.

Satisfied that the arrogant king was off in the village to hear his people bid him a happy birthday, she crossed the courtyard to the kitchen.

A fresh new mural splashed across the once-whitewashed hall, and despite her fear, she glared at the gold painted mural that decked the hall, dotting the more modest blue and pink floral design.

Even their servants had to be surrounded by gold?

It wasn't that she resented them having peace and prosperity – not quite.

But how could she rejoice when they grew their kingdom on the skeletal remains of her own?

They'd not earned their way, and yet the gold of her father's coffers had made their country fat with spoil, and weekly there was more.

King Marc had a taste for riches and pomp.

Spotting the cook, glaring into a boiling caldron, she zigzagged through the busy after-dinner crew.

He scowled when he saw her, sweat beading his red forehead, and his lips curling up at the smell she knew she emitted.

"You are early," he snapped.

"I am." She shrugged, staring back at him evenly, already knowing what he'd say.

"You'll need to wait until I've directed my people before I can show you what skins I have.

She nodded, relieved that her plan had worked. She now had an excuse to loiter.

Hobbling back through the narrow back hall, Arianna broke out into the bright courtyard, limping around the many extra castle folk who were scurrying about.

She tried not to appear suspicious as she headed toward the gardens, but, in her drab dress, she'd look out of place there.

While only the innermost garden, tended by the king himself, was illegal for a commoner to enter, Arianna would have no excuse as to why she would be in any of the gardens, and questions could reveal her mission.

Heart pounding, she gave one quick glance back before stepping through the garden gate.

"Aria!"A voice called from behind.

"Brion." Heart sinking, she turned, and looked down at the glowing seven-year-old with dark, wavy hair like her own.

Like three dozen other children at the castle, Brion was an D'argentian orphan.

There had been more D'argent orphans then homes, and King Marc's solution had been to have many of the children live at the castle and learn trades.

A couple years earlier, Aria had gotten into the habit of bringing pennies to hand to each of the children, and every Wednesday, they surround her like mice, scurrying away once she'd dropped the coins into their outstretched hands. Gifting them pennies had been an impulsive thing to start, but she'd understood their loneliness and wished to do something – even if it was just giving each child a penny.

Admittedly, she had started to regret her habit for slipping around the castle unseen was nary unto impossible with a troop of children always on the lookout for her.

Brion was beaming. "You are early today. I'll tell the others!"

"No! I – don't want you to pull them from their lessons."

He shook his head, smiling wider and revealing two missing teeth. "There are no lessons today. Don't you know it's the king and prince's birthday? Everyone is getting ready!"

"Why aren't you helping?" Arianna asked, wishing he were.

"Oh." He scowled slightly. "Nobody wants me to help. They say I talk too much"

Arianna had thought of the same thing and now to think of how to distract the child and slip into the garden unnoticed, but Brion was smiling again.

"Have you heard of the king's new pet?"

"No." Arianna replied, guessing it was expensive.

"I'm going to go see if I can figure out what it is!"

"I hope you figure it out."

He scampered off, and Arianna looked carefully over the courtyard this time before ducking back through the gate.

In seconds she was out of view of the courtyard, and she let her feet leave the ground, skimming noiselessly over the gravel, hoping no one would smell the stench of the tannery.

She'd washed her dress carefully, but the pungent

smell of the herbs used to make the leather always clung to her clothes.

This was a desperate try, but there were too many legends that led to this one hope and the purpose of her mission.

Somewhere in the gardens, it had long been whispered that there was an ancient door that led in and out of the castle. With the Simmins' ability to read others, it was impossible to get into the castle by trickery so the rebels needed to find the door.

She studied the surroundings. There was much new, but the passage was rumored to have been there for a hundred years. What could be a hundred years old?

Skimming just above the pebbles, Arianna soared the span of the garden, ducking through stone arches.

Prince Marc had ordered the garden renovated. It was still a tenth the size of her father's garden, but it was impressive.

Sectioned into sixteen square courtyards and separated by gravel walkways and walls, each garden section felt like a different world.

One was surrounded by a heavy wall and ivy was being trained to climb around lattices. Another yard was filled with flowers of every color. Still another yard –

A guard's methodical footsteps sounded on the pebbles, and Arianna stilled in her flight.

How close was he? How had she missed his approach?

Pressing back her panic, she flew around the corner of the hedge, sending a whir of wind through the silent garden.

She stopped in midair. Surely, the guard had heard.

Indeed, the guard paused in his step, and she heard him start to double back. Trembling, she silently soared toward the entry into the adjoining garden and slipped through just as she heard his step stop in the opposite door.

Had he seen?

She waited. From her left, she heard more steps.

Her heart leapt to her throat as she looked desperately for a place to hide. Surely there was a tree or bush!

Nay. The gardens had many trees, but this garden plot where she hovered was treeless and instead, a hundred useless daffodils nodded up at her.

One last garden lay closest to the castle, and she knew it was the forbidden one planted with the choicest trees and tended only by the king himself. If someone looked through the windows of the family apartments they'd see her, but what choice did she have?

With all her might, she flew into the last garden, hoping the guards were also not allowed into the inner garden, and finally, she realized it had worked. The steps paused and then marched in other direction until they faded and were gone.

They'd not caught her.

Still trembling, Arianna dared to turn and take in her surroundings.

She stared.

Surely, she had stepped into a dream.

Ivy swept over stone walls and blanketed several arches, dotted with purple and dark blue morning glories.

The afternoon sunlight flicked off the top of a small waterfall that splashed gently into a sparkling stream running the length of the stone-walled garden, and a dozen flower beds dotted the space between deep purple moss walkways.

Large deep-pink lilies rose to her right and bush-like shrubs with huge clusters of light purple flowers nodded softly on her left. Around the garden, like fairies at their work, flitted a dozen or more hummingbirds.

She turned slowly in midair, trying to take it all in at once.

Her father had had gardens, but none had been like this. Her father's gardens had been large and cold with gravel walkways that had cut between unbending stone walls and bushes trimmed into submission, cut into perfect circles and squares framed by symmetrically positioned flower beds.

His gardens had been as mechanical and controlled as the rest of his perfect kingdom, but this place was perfect in its sweet wildness.

Slowly, she flew into the garden's center, carried by the magic of the garden and breathing in a hundred sweet smells.

Could a place have a soul? Surely, this one did.

She lowered herself unto the soft purple moss, wishing all ground was so soft. Surely, then her leg would not pain her so much.

Turning, she took in the rest of the place, trying to force herself out of the hazy dream and back to her task.

As if backing out of a magical fog, Arianna forced herself to focus. Where could a door be?

An old bench made of stone sat in the center of a far wall, its stone so old that it that tiny moss had sunken into its aged surface turning it green, and behind it, framing it was an arch shaped like a large door.

She gazed at the stone arch. This had to be the

magic door. Nothing else in the garden was old enough, but how did it open?

She started toward it, but a movement caught her attention to the left, and she glanced to the side, noticing two new figures in the gate closest to the castle.

The garden had created such a trance, that it took Arianna several seconds to realize that the men were real, and then, as if she'd been thrown into an icy lake on a summer's day, she realized that before her stood the king and the prince.

Heart pounding, she faced the two, dropping quickly into a low bow.

She'd been caught, but worse was the expression on the king's face.

He recognizes me.

CHAPTER 3

Marc had never stared so hard at anything in his life.

Arianna.

Arianna had risen from the dead.

She'd come.

Somehow, he'd known she always would come back to the garden – if he built it. He'd lived it a thousand times in his dreams always whisking her away into his arms, usually flying and laughing.

And now, she was here. She was exactly as he'd imagined Arianna to have looked had she lived: the porcelain face, the dark hair, the perfect nose and full lower lip. She'd finally come.

The girl had bowed and remained bent, her gaze

on the ground though she shouldn't be bowing. She was the same position as he.

But he couldn't stop her. He just stood still, staring, keeping himself from blinking in case she disappeared, knowing that he had to be dreaming but praying desperately that he was not.

"Arianna." He finally dared to whisper.

The girl raised her face, and Marc was hit with her eyes. They were impossibly dark, so much so that he could barely see where the iris ended and the pupil started.

No. Arianna had gold eyes.

"This is Aria, the tanner." Thomis said beside him.

Aria? A nickname? No. This was Arianna – except for the eyes.

Marc debated. Could it be this was *not* Arianna?

The king stared hard into her, and Arianna fought panic.

"Aria, the tanner?" The king repeated slowly. "Is Aria a shortened form of your true name?"

Prince Thomis snorted. "She is Aria the tanner,

brother, and she is trespassing in our royal garden. He turned to Arianna. "This inner garden is strictly forbidden, a law well-known."

"I – I –" She knew the law. Everyone knew it.

"Thomis, do not scare her!" The king snapped, still staring.

"I merely state the law, brother."

"It was a mistake. Forgive me." Arianna whispered, searching her mind for what the punishment would be. She had no idea. She'd feared being found out to be a rebel – but trespassing? What could it be?

The king shook his head. "Of course. It's an easy mistake, and the garden has never had a flower of your beauty."

"Or odor." Prince Thomis added.

The king stopped to glare at his brother, but then he regained himself and smiled, reaching for her again as if to escort her out.

"Your name is just Aria?" He asked for the second time.

She knew it was a ruse. He meant to see if she spoke truth. *Liars.* The Simmins nobility were liars. All of them, especially King Marc.

"Aye." She replied, lifting her hand and forcing her lips into a smile. He'd feel no emotions in her.

But nothing had prepared her for his touch for as his hand closed around hers, her body was encased in warmth and spurts of something in her chest as if she wanted to laugh.

But she hadn't laughed in years. She'd forgotten the feeling until this moment.

She stared at him, meeting his equally surprised gaze.

The warmth twisted between them as he stood, his brow pressed down slightly, and she hoped her face remained calm despite the volley of emotions his hand holding hers drew.

If her face did not give away her fear, she knew he'd not feel anything.

They never could.

"She is – just lost." He said briskly to his sneering brother though his stare had intensified, and his hand closed more tightly around her arm.

Arianna nodded mutely, trying to understand where the warmth was coming from. It felt good. For years, she'd used the wall to protect herself, dousing herself with the feelings that would make her strong, feelings that were often cold and lifeless, but this warmth was something of her childhood, long forgotten, but familiar.

She should want to pull her hand away from her enemy, but instead she'd reached her other hand to touch his hand and was relieved when he added.

"I'll escort the lady to the courtyard."

"*Lady?*" Prince Thomis snapped.

"Aye."

"We did not finish our conversation, *brother.*"

But the king waved his other hand and stepped out into the garden with her.

The cobblestones were harsh on her feet after the moss, but it was the added jolt of joy once they were alone that made her trip.

Where were these feelings coming from?

Cruel curse that tied her to this man and made her feel such kind feelings toward her enemy!

"Forgive me," the king said gently pausing to let her regain her footing as his strong grip held to her tightly. "Did I walk too quickly?"

"No." She grit her teeth, hating to admit weakness, but she had no choice but to explain why she could not walk at a normal pace.

"I have a limp."

"I see."

She glanced up at the warm blue eyes.

"I – I am fine." She whispered fumbling for the reason she hated this man. She did. She hated him.

"Does it cause you pain?" he asked, starting to walk again but much more slowly.

It hurt constantly, but plagues upon her if she ever admitted that to Marc Simmins!

"May I ask what happened to your leg?" He prodded.

"I fell while dancing."

"You can dance?"

The warmth grew and Arianna kept her face forward. Did he also think about their dancing and flying as children?

Surely not, and if he did, it was the curse that tied his soul to hers, making a king of two kingdoms think of childhood folly.

"I was a dancer with the gypsies from Vasilocha, but now I have the tannery."

"You are from Vasilocha?" He stopped, his gaze searching again.

"I grew up in Vasilocha," she lied. "And I traveled with the Vasilochaian gypsies from infancy."

The king was frowning, and Arianna feared he would disagree with her, but finally he smiled, a sweet, impish, unkinglike smile that put her back to being eight-years-old and hiding in the garden with him.

"I think there is more to your story, Aria."

"I assure you there is not," she whispered quickly, wondering for the thousandth time what the Simmins would do if they knew the D'argentian heir still lived. Her existence threatened his throne as much as his threatened hers.

"I'm just a tanner." she added.

The warmth was growing, and she had to stop it.

From deep inside herself, she found the memories she needed. The last time Marc Simmins had held her hand, he'd lied. He'd done the very thing he was doing now, pretending friendship while searching within her.

The anger swelled, mixing with the warmth.

"I just tan skins." She turned and started to walk again.

His voice was amused as he fell into step beside her. "And apparently slip into forbidden places."

"I -" She tried to think of something to respond. "The castle is so – big."

"I know the riches in the castle here must make some dizzy." He said sympathetically in an unintentionally haughty voice.

"Aye."

Dizzy as one about vomit, she finished in her head, reaching deeper into the practiced resentment.

"I've worked on the gardens slowly though I've given into a few splurges here and there."

Or a few dozen, she thought.

I've tried to take the sophistication of D'argent and merge it with Terram's honest realness.

Honest crudeness.

"But," he gestured, "I hope that at the autumn ball,

the D'argentian lords will see the gardens as a symbol that all can be restored.

All will be restored when the balances are even, your line is gone, and your gardens are burned to ash.

He paused suddenly, tipping to look at her, and she hoped her thoughts did not show on her face.

"Did you like the garden?" He asked.

She faltered and then nodded. "Yes." This she could say honestly.

"Someday, maybe my gardens will be the best in the world."

"Methinks that the inner garden is far better than any in the world."

He laughed, a gentle, deep sound that made the warmth enveloping her dance. "Nay. 'Tis obvious you've never seen the palace in D'argent.

"Aye. 'Tis obvious."

He dropped her hand, and the warmth left her instantly, leaving her cold.

Why had he stopped? She blinked through the cold.

"Here is the outer gate." The king gestured.

Arianna nodded and turned away, but before she'd made it across the courtyard, a crowd of children, obviously stirred up by Brion, had come out of the kitchen.

"Aria! Aria!" They shouted.

She felt her face heat as more children poured into the courtyard until two dozen jumped around her while the king watched in amazement.

"The king!" A child's voice called, and they all paused in grabbing at Aria long enough to bob into sloppy bows.

"King Marc!" They cheered.

The king laughed and walked up to their group. "Why are you descending upon this lady like moths to a candle?"

"Aria always brings us pennies, Sire!" Brion smiled, again revealing his top two missing teeth.

Digging her hand quickly into her pockets, Arianna forced herself to smile at them and thrust out the pennies as fast as she could, not caring that some children received several.

The children scampered off, disappearing as fast as they'd come, and Arianna watched them, feeling the king's gaze.

"It's important when you are an orphan to have something that is yours," she explained briskly, feeling the heat cover her neck.

"You are an orphan?" The gentleness in his voice was cruel.

She let out her breath slowly and nodded, angry that her enemy should see her as a crippled orphan and angrier that he cared.

"'Twould seem everyone knows you except me. How have I not met you?"

"I come on Wednesdays."

"Ah. I go to town on Wednesdays, but how have I not seen you at church?"

"I sit in the back." This was a lie. She did not go to church.

"Come to the ball tonight." He demanded suddenly.

She stared at him, imagining going to the ball, limping in her old, smelly peasant dress. It was a horrible picture. "I don't like balls, and I no longer dance."

He studied her, his blue eyes intense. She thought he was not going to accept her answer, but after several seconds, he nodded.

"Then I will see you next Wednesday."

Of course, he'd not let this go.

"You go to town on Wednesday."

"And now I shall start going on Thursday," he said with decisiveness. "For I shall see you on Wednesday."

She nodded, feeling stunned, and then gave a quick curtsy before heading again toward the kitchen as fast as her leg allowed, trying to weigh all the disasters of the day in her mind.

The king stood and watched her limp the entire

rest of the way across the courtyard before she ducked into the hot kitchen.

Soul connection or not, did the fool have to be so obvious?

Foolish man!

Amazing woman.

Marc stared at the kitchen door, sorry she was gone from his view.

Here, on his twenty-first birthday, he'd met the first woman he'd been interested in since Arianna.

Maybe a tanner but certainly a princess at heart. How else had she stood bravely before him e'en after being caught? A lesser woman would have withered, but not her.

And to think that she gave so generously to the orphans!

Sweet, lovely, generous woman. He smiled to himself. *And she was in my garden.*

He never let anyone in that garden. It was his place alone, but it had almost been as if –

She belonged there, he thought.

'Twas as if she belonged in his most private place.

He stood dazedly by the gate his mind whirling.

But how was it that he couldn't read her?

Never had he touched someone and not been able to read them. How was it even possible?

She did seem to be a very calm person. 'Twas possible she did not feel much, but even when she was found trespassing by the king himself? How could she not have felt some fear? She'd looked frightened -

"Methinks she's bewitched you." Thomis' voice behind him interrupted Marc's thoughts.

Marc turned. "If it's an enchantment, I like it."

"And it makes you act the fool with a woman who has no position, no education, no family, absolutely no conversation skills, and whose smell heralds her presence half an hour before she arrives."

Marc laughed. "The smell is not so bad!"

Thomis sniffed. "It will fill my nostrils the rest of the day. The garderobe smells better. You know there is a reason they put the tannery at the edge of the town."

Marc chuckled, walking back into the garden, but Thomis continued. "I have heard the tanners use repulsive smelling herbs – and sometimes worse things - on the leather, but by the saints, I think she douses herself with it."

Marc laughed. "But did you see how pretty she was?"

"She has a pleasant face –"

"Pleasant? She's beautiful! I could barely breathe for the sight of her."

"Or because of the odor."

Marc shook his head. "I must know more about her."

Thomis snorted. "She's just the tanner, and if I remember rightly, before that she was in some circus."

"You do know about her!"

Thomis sighed impatiently. "Of course. I know of everyone we do business with because I must watch our accounts while you buy overpriced geladas, but concerning the girl, there's not much to know. She came here a few years ago with a group of traveling gypsies, but she'd fallen while performing. They left her here though one fellow stayed and started that little minstrel company that travels around."

Marc tightened.

Casimir. He knew the man and had had his eye on him for a long time. Aria had traveled with him? Surely, she'd not known him well.

"And what of Aria? How did she become a tanner?" he asked.

"Well, the old tanner received a mysterious letter

offering a large sum to train the girl and leave her the tannery."

Marc was astounded he'd not heard of this. "By whom?"

"That was the strangest thing. The letter was signed by that woman that was always helping over in D'argent during the war. You know, the one rumored to be magic? Laelynn."

Marc didn't speak for several seconds. He *had* heard of Laelynn. She had been an ongoing legend around D'argent during the years of war. It had been said that whenever there was a great need, she would appear.

"I can't believe I did not know of this." He mused.

"Well, mayhap you were too busy planting flowers, brother."

Marc smirked. "Well, tell me all your mind. Hold nothing back."

"All of it?" Thomis did not see the humor. "I've much more to speak to you then, brother. I think you are using the money poorly, Marc. You build gardens when you should build alliances and trade routes. It angers me that you are not focusing on trade *west-ward*. We have the funds now to open a pass. We can't just depend on one trade route to our east if we can open a second."

Marc sighed. His short break with the mysterious tanner was over, and he once again had to focus on matters of state.

"We are not strong enough, Thomis. I need to keep building alliances with the lords of the east kingdom and the Jade Isles before I divide my resources to build west."

"But maybe if we started, the king of the west kingdom would help us build the routes we need. Right now, we depend on this tenuous peace between the last eastern lords of D'argent and the Jade Isles."

"A peace that I built."

"Aye, but it's a peace that you can't keep – not with just charm and wit while you put your resources to making flower gardens. And you plan to sign a contract with dragon's blood? It shows you are desperate."

Usually, it was always fun to anger Thomis. His brother pretended no feeling, but when he was angered by an argument, his nostrils would flare, and the angrier Thomis became, the more Thomis looked like a skinny, angry bull.

"You want peace as well, Thomis."

"But dragon's blood? Do you forget the stories, brother? Dragons are deceivers, liars, luring you to your doom!"

Marc burst out laughing. "We have its blood, brother. It's dead. What is there to fear from a dead dragon?"

Thomis' nose had deformed so much, he looked like he could oink, but instead he snapped. "You are being a fool!"

Marc crossed his arms. "It is you who would divide our resources. The only reason that the Ecoptians and the Jade Isle pirates leave us in peace is that I have most of our soldiers in forts along the coast. Even if I did take some money to build a route west, I can't take the men from the forts."

Thomis was angrier then he'd been in years. His nose had taken on new shape. Marc was pleased. It served his brother right for his rudeness to Aria, the tanner. "I've done the math, but to hope that you can keep this tentative peace on our eastern side is folly." He said.

"Stick to your chess, brother." Marc smiled, starting to turn away.

Thomis grabbed Marc's arm. "Let me go to the king of the west. A percentage to contribute to the road is all I'm asking."

His brother was earnest. Doubt clouded Marc's mind. Was he wrong? Maybe it would be wise to send a percentage to trying other options.

The wind lifted the hanging vines on the wall behind his brother.

Something about it reminded him of his flight long ago with Arianna.

How he wished he could build a kingdom like the D'argentian kingdom had been before the war, to be as great and powerful as King Thrush himself.

Marc caught himself. "No." He croaked.

"No? Thomis glowered. "We have no money to build alliances but must you buy plants and jewels – and this, this creature from our enemies? We could sell out some of the treasure."

"Treasure?"

"Yes. Empty that tower room where you hoard the Thrush heirlooms."

Marc shook his head. "Those are the heirlooms of the Thrush family."

He thought of a beautiful crown, 120 diamonds that had been planned for Arianna had she lived. And the throne, plated in gold and studded in rubies, that the great king Thrush had sat on in all his glory.

Thomis' voice was quiet. "Do not hold onto things that will never be, brother."

Marc shook his head. "There will be peace soon, brother, and then the Thrush treasures will be brought back to D'argent as they should be. They cannot be sold. They are precious to the people of D'argent."

Thomis gasped in exasperation. "People that would turn against us if they had the opportunity. We must strengthen our alliances. Don't you see? The Thrush family is dead, brother. *She* is dead, brother."

Marc rarely was given to anger, but it rushed on him instantly.

How dare Thomis try to bring Arianna's memory into a political discussion. The child that died in purity and light should never be talked about for political gain.

Thomis had overstepped, and Marc saw from his brother's pale face that he knew it, but Thomis didn't back down. "I heard you call the tanner 'Arianna' earlier, brother. You must stop looking for the dead, Marc."

Marc had to push out the words between gritted teeth. "There will be no road, Thomis, as long as I am king. We will work for the people of Terram and D'argent. We will make a peace treaty with the Jade Isles, and we have plenty of other gold to do it.

Marc waited for his brother's nostrils to flare. Maybe Thomis would be so angry, his lips would do something too. But instead, Thomis went completely still, straightening slowly and stepping back, his poise perfect.

"Very well, brother." Thomis said quietly, his tone as frozen as his expression. Then he turned and strode away.

Marc forced himself to stay still and not to try to stop him. They would never agree on this, and Thomis had to accept that Marc was king and not Thomis.

CHAPTER 4

The smells of honey and spices mixed with the scent of mid-summer blossoms as Marc tried to comb his wavy hair back into submission.

To think, he'd always dreaded this birthday.

All was as he'd planned, and now, he could just enjoy his birthday!

A knock sounded at the door, and Marc laughed when he saw who was there.

Petir!

"You look well, sire." The broad physician strode into the solar, Marc's personal room, and Marc clapped the physician on the back, thankful for his old friend, the man who had helped Marc more than anyone else he knew.

"I'm glad you've finally come home to Terram. You belong here."

"I'm thankful to be back in Terram, sire."

"Happy birthday, brother." Thomis scowled in the door where Petir had just been.

Marc looked past Petir to Thomis. "And to you, *twin* brother. You cannot still be angry over earlier! You could attempt a smile on our birthday!"

Thomis swallowed, his eyes sliding to the side. "The burgesses have come to wish you birthday tidings."

Marc crossed the room. "What a friendly gesture!"

But when they entered the great hall, the burgesses didn't look friendly.

Burgess Tinman was staring at his feet. "We came to wish Your Majesty and - and Prince Thomis a happy birthday."

"Well, we thank you." Marc smiled, but he was the only one smiling.

The man shifted. "And then when we came in, we started to talk about the – law."

Which law? *The law?*

Marc shook his head. "Yes, that foolish old law – dead as it was foolish."

"N- no, Sire, the law that is much alive right now."

Alive?

Marc tried to think what they meant.

The men were exchanging looks, none of them wishing to speak.

Marc decided to choose one.

"Burgess Tinman, what is this about?"

"Well – that is to say, we realized you must obey the law."

The man started to speak faster, his eyes flitting to avoid Marc's stare. "You must marry – tonight – or – or in accordance with the law, you must forfeit to Prince Thomis."

"But he isn't married either!" Marc gasped. They could not be serious.

"Actually brother, I'd have another year since there is a clause in the law for having attained the throne so close to my twenty-first birthday."

Marc waved his hand. "I can't marry tonight!"

"If I may offer my daughter -" Tinman started

"I also have one about the right age – just a few years older than yourself," interrupted another burgess.

"A *few* years older?" retorted Burgess Tinman. "She's nearly thirty."

"Twenty-nine only."

Marc shook his head, grabbing the nearest

burgess' arm. The man's feelings had changed – completely.

Marc reached for another, not even hiding his desperation. Again, all was changed.

How? It was impossible. He'd been so careful for months, sowing flattery and convincing them all.

How in a matter of hours?

But it didn't matter he realized as he gaped at the stony faces.

He had to marry; he had no choice.

Marriage.

The word rang in his head like an executioner's drum.

Marc strode fast with Thomis through the garden, his mind numb.

"The priest is attending the ball. I shall send a page to bring him to the church. You have less than three hours, now, brother."

Marc nodded.

Something the size of a small human darted across the walk in front of them.

In his haze, he thought it was just a fitting addition to the nightmare he was in for it was so ugly, it could well have hobbled out of a nightmare, but as it paused, raising on its haunches to stare at him, he realized it was an animal.

"What is that?" Marc demanded.

It was the ugliest creature he'd ever seen, a baboon, with fluffy straw-brown hair and a black face. It darted up the walk – coming to rest on a large rock.

"I've been told this is your birthday present to yourself, your gelada."

It curled its lips back into a heinous expression that revealed massive eye teeth, and Marc tripped back.

But the creature was not threatening. It tipped up on its hind legs, looking curiously at him.

"It's smiling at you," Thomis goaded dryly.

His brother crossed his arms. "I see two monkeys, and it's clear which is the more clever for he is the one smiling."

Marc shrugged, stalking past the animal. "I'm smiling, brother. I get to marry tonight."

"And who will that be?"

They were passing the inner garden, and Marc smiled, thinking of the pretty tanner standing their earlier. He paused in the door of the inner garden, remembering finding her there like a lost fairy.

"I can think of good a choice," Marc said, starting to feel better about the marriage.

"Aye. There is only one." Thomis nodded emphatically.

"Really?"

Marc had expected Thomis to have a list in order of dowry and alliance.

"What choice is that?"

"Lillian, the governor's daughter of course. A princess with a larger dowry would have been better, but Lillian is the best we could do in three hours."

Marc laughed. "Lillian? She only talks of parties."

"Which you love to schedule."

"And she just sits about being waited on by servants."

"Of which you have many."

"She talks incessantly."

"Aye. She is social and adept."

Marc threw up his hands. "You want the alliance with her father. That is why you want this union!"

Thomis nodded vigorously. "Of course, that is why! What other purpose is there that we must discuss?"

Marc laughed. "You play my life and happiness like a chess board."

"And play it well, brother."

Marc shook his head. "I think I have a better idea."

"Which is?"

"Aria."

Thomis frowned. "Is she one of the diplomat's daughters?"

Marc gestured toward the inner garden, and Thomis' face opened in surprise.

"*Smelly* Aria? She lives in the *tannery*!"

"And once I marry her, she'll live in the castle. She's the only interesting woman I know. Can you imagine how dull Lillian would be?"

Thomis was gaping at him. "But the tannery – and - and she smells."

"Well, when we marry, she'll take a bath."

"Certainly, you are not serious. She never smiles."

"Well, not at you"

"Nor at you!"

That was true, but Marc shrugged. "Of course, she was frightened. I am the king. She was just afraid of me."

"No one is afraid of you!"

Marc scoffed. "You really just want her to have a dowry."

"Of course, I do! You spend a lot of money, and we are already weak. Be serious, Marc. She is just a tanner!"

Marc started to turn away, but Thomis grabbed Marc's hand. "Lillian is the better choice. She's the daughter of the governor. You'd be the governor's son and keep a good alliance."

Marc stilled. He did love his kingdom, and he knew it needed a good alliance.

A good alliance. Yes.

Was he being foolish? Aye, he was. Marc sighed. "Perhaps, you are right."

Thomis nodded. "Obviously, I'm right. We need money. You know we do. With things as precarious as they are, the Nobilis fortune will give you what you need to strengthen your allies. There really is no other choice."

Marc looked up at the night sky. A thousand stars laughed at him. He was as bound to his fate as each star, unable to move or even marry for love. This was why he'd put off the marriage. He knew there was no other choice, and as unhappy as it made him, he had to accept it.

Of course. There is no other choice. I need that money to build our kingdom.

Thomis smiled, dropping his hand from Marc's arm. "I'll make the arrangements, brother."

Thomis disappeared in the direction of the ball, and Marc headed toward his chamber, his mind whirling. Tonight, he'd be married to Lillian Nobilis.

She was pretty, and she'd grown up in far more luxury than most in their war-torn kingdom. She'd know how to handle the servants and plan parties. But mostly, he needed the money their marriage would bring. There was no other choice. It was a good alliance.

There is no other choice.

In an hour he'd be married.

In a year, he could have a child.

Children.

His family always had twins. Thomis and his brother, his father and Uncle Amis – and a dozen generations back.

If he weren't feeling so grim, he'd even smile imagining spoiled Lillian balancing twins, but instead, he stopped to frown.

Lillian would pass their children off to servants; of that he was confident.

He walked to the window that overlooked the courtyard, remembering how the children had gathered around Aria.

She would never toss her children off to others to raise.

Aria. The fathomless dark eyes, the grace in the way she could walk despite the limp -

"What am I doing?" He gasped to the empty room. "Why, I know exactly who I wish to marry."

He laughed. Praise be to the One Father for clearing his foggy head before he made a terrible mistake!

Through the halls, down the stairs and out to the stable, he raced, relieved to see that the six soldiers were still mounting their horses.

Marc strode into the stable. "Halt! Do not you go to the governor's mansion. My bride lives at the tannery! Fetch her quickly!"

The men gaped at him. Did they not know who he was referring to?

"Go, men! Bring Aria the Tanner to the church. Tell her I must marry, and I've chosen her."

Marc strode back into the castle. What would Aria think of this news? He wished he could have told her himself.

It would surprise her of course, but it would be a most pleasant surprise. Joyful, wondrous.

She would be delighted. Marrying him was what every girl in the kingdom wanted.

If there was one thing Marc knew, it was that everyone loved him.

If there was one thing Arianna knew, it was that she hated King Marc.

It had taken so little – a touch – a bit of mercy and a few kind words, and she was thinking of him again!

"Don't be a fool, Arianna." She whispered.

She steeled herself, playing though her mind all he'd done to her until the rage iced over any memory of the warmth that had filled her when they'd touched.

The warmth! Oh, sweet warmth, refreshing like soft rain on a summer afternoon –

Nay! She could not think of him. He was her enemy.

And his family -

"I heard they saw you!"

The door swung open, and Casimir stalked into the small tanner's cottage.

Aria pushed aside the skin she was scraping.

"It – it was alright. The king let me go –"

"He found out?"

She swallowed. "I – yes. I – the door – there *is* a door, but it is in his personal garden."

"The king saw you?" Casimir paled.

She sighed and avoided Casimir 's gaze as she picked the skin back up and began scraping again. "I promise he did not plan to punish me; he suspected nothing. He said as much."

Casimir scoffed, and Arianna dropped the skin, limping past him to the dark outer yard where her caldron bubbled, boiling a skin for tanning.

He followed her, but to her relief, he was calming.

"Do not fear," he said quietly staring into the caldron as it bubbled. "We will bring down the house of Simmins.

She didn't respond, but increasingly, she feared he was wrong.

It had been easy to hope when she'd had strength, when she'd danced before the people and they'd loved her e'en while she plotted against them.

But now she had no strength. She had a limp, and she had a tannery that she had to work hard to keep.

Casimir had strength and therefore had hope.

She had none.

The fury in the land that had continually stirred under the surface was gone. Even the D'argentians were ready to move forward and become willing subjects to the people of Terram in the name of peace, and this new treaty could seal the D'argentian's fate forever. If it brought the peace promised, there would be no more disagreement between the kingdoms.

Everyone hoped — though she was sure everyone feared — it was too wonderful to be true.

And they were right. It was too wonderful. She wanted blood, a small payment for all the bloodshed the Simmins had caused.

Casimir was scowling. "I fear he will still retaliate against you."

It was so much worse than he could guess. Their mortal enemy was close to guessing her identity, and while after today, she knew Marc wouldn't hurt her, what of his family?

As she had dozens of times before, she debated telling Casimir her greatest secret, her true identity.

She took a hesitant step forward, but as he looked up at her, she saw the deadly protectiveness in his gaze, and she turned back to the caldron.

"He will not retaliate." She whispered, stirring the skin in the caldron, but like a bad omen, her words were met with the shaking of the earth.

Slowly, she turned as several horses broke through the treeline, and on their backs were soldiers wearing the color of the Simmins.

Surely, it was nothing, a misunderstanding, but her own terror froze her to the ground.

They'd found her. Had someone seen her fly? Did they know who she was?

Cold as ice, she dropped the paddle back into the pot as the guards dismounted.

"You're wanted at the church."

Church?

She shook her head in confusion.

The soldier's face was stoic.

"The king must marry by midnight. He's chosen you."

She couldn't move, scrambling for connections. She'd heard he'd have to marry, but somehow, he'd been able to skirt the law –

But he hadn't, and he'd chosen her.

That was the only part that made sense of this. Unbeknownst to Marc, she had somehow connected their souls. She still didn't know how she'd done it, but with their souls connected, he could only choose her.

And she wouldn't tell him - not now, not when she was the last of her line.

She stared, the fullness of the opportunity hitting her. As queen of their kingdom, she could finally help her people.

"She will not be forced to marry." Casimir pushed past her, standing in the midst of the soldiers, but he wasn't looking at the soldiers. He was looking toward the caldron that sat on the blazing fire in the yard.

"I – I must obey the king." She grabbed Casimir's gaze.

Obviously, he'd understand the opportunity she'd

have, and surely, he would see this was best for the cause.

But he took a step toward the caldron. "No subject must be forced against their will to obey tyranny!"

He was normally so careful. Didn't he realize the danger?

She again tried to get catch his eye, but he had raised his palms in the direction of the boiling water and flickering flames.

Did he mean to use force? Arianna panicked.

"You claim peace because you hold a sword to our backs," he yelled boldly. "And now, the arrogant cumberwalt of a king thinks he can take a woman by force and marry her against her will? She'll never have him."

He took two more steps toward the caldron. Arianna realized she'd only have seconds. She'd have to make her move while soldiers were focused on Casimir.

Carefully she directed the air to hit the caldron, dropping it off the tripod and into the flames, spilling its contents and extinguishing the flame as well as soaking the ground with the water.

Casimir turned and started to raise his hands, but she threw herself forward, bumping into him. "Please Casimir! It will be alright!"

Casimir had to grab her to steady himself, but what Arianna hadn't foreseen was that the soldiers would use those same seconds to grab Casimir from behind.

"No! I'll come!" Arianna screamed. "Let him go!"

But the commander ignored her.

"Take him to the castle!" He snapped.

The soldiers paused in confusion. Prisoners were usually housed in the small town prison and guarded by a single deputy.

But the commander motioned to his men. "Do you not hear his accent and see his hate? This is a rebel, not a mere common peasant. He will be tried before the king."

Arianna was shaking. She'd never have guessed that they'd arrest Casimir. She had thought she'd avoided trouble not caused it. Now she had no choice at all. She had to marry the king and use her position to gain Casimir 's freedom.

Casimir was struggling against the two soldiers that held him, and he was overpowering them, but as Arianna watched, a third soldier drew his sword.

"No! Don't kill him!" Arianna raised her hand to knock the soldier down with the air, but before she could, the soldier had driven the hilt down on Cassimer's head. Her friend slumped to the ground, unconcious.

In seconds, she'd been dragged up onto a horse and clasped against a soldier with bad breath. Before she could see what happened to Casimir, the horse was galloping into the woods and the trees were blurring around her.

CHAPTER 5

*A*rianna was going to marry her enemy, Marc Simmins.

Her mind whirled, but she could not catch her thoughts before they'd arrived in town and were passing through the church's double doors.

And then she was inside, and there were several more knights, a few officials, all the burgesses, and at the very front of the church was the king, splendidly dressed, a stark contrast to her drab brown skirt.

Someone was pushing her now, and she was at the front of the church.

"Seven minutes, Sire!" A fat burgess with a full beard burst out as Arianna came to a halt across from the king.

The king ignored the burgess focusing only Arianna. "Are you alright? I know this is sudden."

She nodded though it wasn't sudden at all. She'd sealed their fate when they were eight.

His blue eyes were searching hers, and he reached for her hand. "Are you - happy with the union?"

Arianna held her palms flat against her skirts, forcing her voice to stay steady. "I was just told I'll be a queen. Of course, I am pleased."

"Aye, we can tell by your smile," Prince Thomis snapped sarcastically from the king's side.

The prince turned, gesturing to a man who darted to the back of the church and then up the ladder to the clock and bell tower, and Arianna focused back on the king.

"I am pleased you accepted." The king said, his usual intense stare making it difficult to meet his gaze.

She nodded, and then the priest began reading from the black book, but she couldn't think of what he was saying. All she could think was that she marrying her enemy. She was marrying Marc Simmins.

And then they had all stopped, and they were looking at her, and she realized she was to say something.

This was the vows. She was to vow something.

She needed to do this for her people.

"Ugh - Yes." She nodded, unable to remember the last time she was at a wedding. She'd never had a desire to go; romance was a lie as were most of the follies that the people of Terram loved and celebrated.

"You do?" The priest prodded.

She looked across at Marc Simmins, the man who symbolized all that she hated; he was glowing, absolutely and completely glowing.

He didn't know about the soul curse. He didn't know they were connected, and that he had no choice. He thought he was choosing.

In his pride, he thought he was in control and the world would not fall spinning off course in the span of a second, and she, Princess Arianna Thrush, was the one who was going to destroy his world.

Finally, she'd have enough power to ruin him.

"I do." She heard herself say, and she meant it.

The priest nodded and began speaking again - slower, and slower.

Marc had not remembered that there was supposed to be such a long speech between each of the vows. This should be so much quicker, and even if it were required for the marriage, couldn't they make an exception? It was very close to midnight now.

He'd been worried before they'd finally brought her, pacing outside the church and stopping repeatedly to look up at the huge clock that hung from the steeple. It was wound every twelve hours by large gears in an inner room, and it ticked mercilessly toward midnight.

But then they'd come with seven minutes to spare!

Now, if the priest would simply hurry!

He stared across at Aria.

She was incredibly beautiful, even in her rough dress and the tight bun she always wore. He could hardly wait to buy her silks – one of every color and velvet – dark black to match her eyes if he could find some black enough.

The priest started reading an exhortation always given to newlyweds which Marc had also forgotten about having to be part of the ceremony.

Marc tried to stay patient, studying the lovely woman in front of him.

Her response had been puzzling.

Joy would have made sense. He was the king after all! And everyone liked him. Every woman wished to marry him as well — as this one of course.

The soldiers standing on either side of her made

her look a bit like a prisoner, but of course she wasn't. She came by choice. He was sure she was delighted – only surprised.

Though - she hadn't look surprised – nor particularly pleased.

Uncomfortable, Marc looked back at the priest. Why was it taking the priest so long?

"Please hurry." He broke in. "We've so little time."

The priest raised his brows. "Two minutes, Sire."

Thomis pulled at the priest, turning him to the side and murmuring in ear.

Thanks for Thomis, trying to help move it along!

But was it possible? The priest spoke slower!

"Do you vooooow ...to the Ooone Father... to loooooove and cherish her for as loooooong as yoooou live?

"I do."

Marc meant it. He vowed to her, and to the One Father. He would love her, and it seemed an impossible vow to break. How could he not love this beautiful young woman in front of him? After all of his misgivings and putting off marriage, Marc found the vow to be the easiest and most natural thing in the world.

"Then by the authority given by the One Father, you are husband and wife."

Husband and wife. Marc reached for her, but she didn't move forward.

Instead, she held out a pale hand, and he took it.

Nothing. He could feel nothing at all, not even a tremor. This woman was made of iron!

Her fingers were not soft in his. They were calloused, but her hand was small, and he squeezed it trying to encourage her.

'Twas obvious she was not ready for a kiss so he'd not ask it.

"Very well. Now, back to the castle." Marc announced, wondering if there were any guests left at the castle's birthday ball for him to present his new bride to.

The priest was whispering with Thomis and now cleared his throat, his face suddenly as white as his hair.

"Forgive me, Your Majesty. 'Twas 12:01 – almost 12:02 when we finished."

Marc couldn't think what he meant.

"You said we had two minutes."

"And three you took."

Marc shook his head. "Well, no matter."

"The church upholds the law of the land, Sire, and that matters." The priest was looking toward Thomis instead of Marc.

Marc frowned. He could command the priest to

change the time, but then he checked himself. The priest didn't answer to the crown; he answered to the Church. The church had a different hierarchy than Terram, and Marc was powerless against it.

But surely, the priest was wrong! They'd had seven minutes when she arrived. They'd not taken that long.

Marc strode out the door, twisting to look up at the big clock.

How was it possible?

12:02

He blinked up at it, confident that this was some mistake.

And what would this mean for him? A fine? A kind of penance?

A greater penalty niggled at the back of his mind, but it was preposterous.

He turned back, and the expressions of his soldiers said what Marc could not mentally grasp.

He turned to the burgesses; they all stood stoically, their faces also sad.

"Oh, come now!" Marc laughed.

Thomis shook his head. "Brother, the law is the law. If you had not tried to skirt it, you'd not have accidentally broken it."

"I – I didn't break the law. 'Twas the priest who droned on and on! I was here and ready to marry."

Thomis sighed. "It's a lie to claim you didn't break the law when you did. If it weren't for your arrogance -"

"My arrogance! You'd condemn me over a single minute?" Marc started to heat.

Marc looked again to his people. Their expressions ranged between sorrow and shock.

Would anyone step forward for him?

Marc fought to think of what to do. This was escalating, but he didn't know how to stop it.

Surprisingly, it was his new wife who spoke out beside him, her voice clear and slicing. "This is betrayal within the house of Simmins and against your own flesh and blood." His petit bride limped forward, glaring up at Thomis.

Her words made Thomis tense and his nostrils flare slightly, but then he raised his voice. "Betrayal is when the king tries to manipulate the law according to his own purpose. The law said he had to marry by midnight, and he tried to use his influence to avoid obeying the law. 'Tis obvious he pushed too far and now, he's fallen into his own trap."

Marc scoffed but could not think how to respond. Hadn't these burgesses been the men he'd bribed and coddled for months? There was too much truth to Thomis' speech. The burgesses shifted, and Marc saw their faces harden.

Thomis marched out of the church. "The night is over. To your homes."

"Wait, brother!" Marc yelled, jogging after him. But before Marc reached the street, Thomis had pulled up onto a horse, and by the time Marc made it out into the street, his brother was gone.

Like useless tin soldiers, obeying what they were told, the burgesses and castle knights filed out of the church.

Marc raced around to each one. "Come now, Thimnis! Caspir?"

Each avoided his gaze, and as Marc felt them, their hearts beat with resolve – though each was sorry.

No one would stand for him? Not a one?

The priest was glowering in the doorway of the church. "'Twas not *I* that broke the law." He huffed and slammed the church doors shut with a heavy thud.

And suddenly, Marc found himself out in the warm night standing alone beside his bride trying to understand the ridiculousness of what just happened.

"I will set this right in the morning." Marc told her.

She looked away, and he waited, confused again at her eerie calm.

Finally, she turned back, her tone as cold as her expression. "It's a half an hour walk to the tannery."

Marc nodded as he considered possibilities.

"Thomis was angry at me earlier, and he's probably trying to teach me a lesson. I assume this is some form of prank or something. It's all moves with him, but I suppose he may view it as a bit of a chess game."

"'Twould seem he has won it," she replied.

"No. I think he just – ugh took a pawn or something."

"It appears he has the castle, the crown, and all the pawns." She started to walk away toward the direction of the tannery.

Marc didn't know what else to do but to head there with her though they had to walk slowly because of her limp, and as they walked, Marc found himself ranting.

"Traitors! Hoodlums! Rats. To think after all I've done, they'd treat me thus!"

His wife didn't speak a single word. If it weren't for the soft dragging of her bad heel, he'd have thought he was walking alone.

He couldn't stop his tirade to see how she felt about it. Obviously, she agreed. They'd both been betrayed – though the betrayal to him was far worse for he'd been a king and she a mere tanner. "I'll sort this out tomorrow, of course. I assure you this will not stand. I'll appeal to -"

Who? He wasn't sure, but he'd get it all sorted out.

"I'll find a way to make this right. 'Tis just a mis-understanding. All will be well soon!"

She didn't respond, and her silence made him nervous that she didn't believe him.

It was three quarters of an hour before they reached the tannery and while it was too dark to see, he knew the place by the smell.

He stumbled into the dank cottage, tripping over the cold, stone floor, feeling around and knocking over a stool and hitting his knee against a table.

"'Tis mad that anyone would live here," he snapped.

Finally, he found the alcove on the side wall and realized it was a bed, closed behind a large wooden cabinet door.

He pushed his hand over the rough fabric, straw poking his fingers from underneath. He was spending his wedding night in a dank cabin that stunk of strong herbs and leather.

Arianna hated it when men were angry.

She remembered the servants cowering when her father would rage though it hadn't stopped her father beating them. At the time, she had thought herself safe from a man's anger, but then had come the circus and the endless months of low business as the D'argentian war had reached its icy fingers over to Vasilocha. By day, the head gypsy would smile and joke and perform for the crowds only to yell at her and the other performers later in the woods when they'd barely brought in enough to buy a meager supper.

Now, she steeled herself, edging back toward the open door as she watched the king's anger grow as he took in the cottage.

The more he saw, the quieter he became, and she waited. Next would come the explosion.

He had stopped by the bed and was staring at it, and she gingerly felt for the open door, finding it behind her.

But then, she saw him deflate and his shoulders lower.

"This was not the wedding night I had planned," the king said quietly.

He turned, his expression sad. "But we should sleep."

Together?

"I – must close the chickens up for the night." She lied. She'd put the chickens in their little shelter hours ago.

"I saw no chickens out." He motioned toward the bed, and Arianna took an involuntary step back.

"I see," He snapped, his gaze piercing even in the dark. "Very well then. See to the chickens."

Arianna jumped out of the cottage, closing the door behind her and letting the cool night air wear off the shock enough to realize what the last two hours had held.

She'd married Marc Simmins only to be betrayed again by the Simmins.

And what of Casimir? She needed to help him escape. If he was tried by Thomis, she would not put it past Thomis to make an example of Casimir.

But how? She could not think of how to help him except to break into the castle, but that was dangerous. She wouldn't dare. Would she?

Arianna waited almost an hour before slipping back in to the cottage. Silently as she could, she lay a thin blanket in the corner where she'd had a pile of straw she'd planned to make into a rush rug and finally lay down, listening to the king toss and turn on her little bed.

How many nights had she dreamed to see her enemies fall? Too many to count.

Now her greatest enemy, the king of the country that had killed her family and drove her from her rightful place had fallen, and Arianna was at the perfect vantage point to watch his misery.

She should be enjoying it. She had every right to, but she could not help but think of him standing in the middle of the village street, his face open in confusion as everyone he trusted walked away and left him there. She'd known what he was feeling; she'd felt it once herself -

No! Don't be a fool! His family took everything from me, and now he even takes my bed. She chided herself.

Pushing her face into the straw, she let it poke into her cheek until it hurt.

The pain was enough to strengthen against any foolish feelings. Tomorrow, she'd find a way into the castle and figure out how to save Casimir, and no matter how pathetic Marc Simmins was, she'd not forget that he was still her enemy.

Resolved, she went to sleep.

Marc's sleep had come quickly, but so did the nightmares.

He was running up and down the village's main

street, and the people kept asking him why he'd abandoned them.

But he hadn't!

They'd abandoned him – even after all he'd done.

And then, Marc woke to find that the nightmare was real. He had woken in a tannery.

By daylight, he saw that his original assessment of the cottage had been harsh.

As a cottage, it was better than most.

It had high ceilings with strong, thick beams stretching across what could be a second story if it were built, but instead, it stretched up, making the cottage feel spacious.

The stone floor was clean while white walls swept up to a large hearth where a tripod and black kettle sat.

In the opposite corner were several shelves that included pots and baskets though no books, not even the book of the One Father that was in almost every home.

Still, there was something odd about the cottage —though he could not think what. It was perfectly clean and organized, but something was missing.

Maybe he was wrong. Every utilitarian item was there - baskets of every size stacked beside two huge chests, pots, neat butter churn, a broom, a chair and stool, a bare table, and even a spinning wheel.

Why did it feel as if something were missing?

He stood, looking around for his petite bride. Had she slept in the small bed with him?

Marc staggered toward the open door, his stiff legs showing how much they'd missed his feather bed.

Even the early morning, heat hung in the thick air, and he saw Aria adding to the heat with a bubbling caldron almost the size of herself which she was stirring with a long paddle. She must have been up for a while for dark tendrils of hair had fallen from her bun and curled around her downturned face.

"What do we eat here?" He asked. He'd meant to be charming, but it was hard to be gentle when he had woken to so much wrong done to him.

She tipped her head toward another boiling pot.

"Excellent. The day isn't hot enough. Why have one boiling pot when you could have two?"

She raised a dark brow, not lifting her eyes from the pot.

"Would you rather have what's in here?" She pointed to the foul-smelling pot.

The dark eyes raised, and Marc was hit with her, but resisting the distraction, he stalked past her, lifting the ladle to study the murky broth.

"Where is the meat that goes with the skins?"

She choked back a laugh. "Not to my table."

Marc dropped the ladle back into the muddy-colored mixture. "What kind of existence is this?"

Her humor died instantly. "The kind that survives."

Turning quickly, she limped toward the woodpile at the side of the yard.

For a fraction of a breath, he wondered if he should help, but he hardened himself to it.

He was not born for this; it was all a mistake.

He needed to go speak to Thomis. This was a ridiculous misunderstanding.

Her arms piled high with wood, Arianna watched Marc stomp toward the tree line.

Where was he going?

The door. She knew instantly. If it existed, he'd go through it.

She needed to know where that door was – for the rebels – and for Casimir.

Dropping the wood, she flew quickly, following him at a distance.

Would he really? Of course –

Heart pounding, she forced herself to pull back,

careful to keep far enough back that he'd not sense her presence, but she needn't have worried.

He was far too focused, his gaze straight ahead, his steps turned away from the town –

He's going to the cemetery. She realized.

That she'd not thought of it was laughable for there, at the edge of a hundred ancient graves, pressed into the side of the hill was a huge stone that looked more door-like than like a headstone.

The king didn't even stop in his stride for before his fingers could even brush the surface, the door began to glow, splitting open for him, and though she was still far, she saw that the tunnel was indeed also stone – and also glowing as far into the hill as she could see.

He passed quickly, the still-glowing door swinging silently shut behind him, and by the time, Arianna had flown down, even the intricately-carved lines along the front of the stone had stopped glowing.

She dropped unto the mossy ground, studying the door.

Had he spoken? She'd been too far to hear. What had caused it to open?

She ran her fingers along the thick stone, knowing instinctively that it could not be broken.

"Open!" She commanded.

Nothing.

She grimaced but pushed the words out. "Open for the – wife of - of Simmins."

Nothing moved in the cemetery except a few birds in the overgrown trees overhead.

The door would not open for her.

Drawing in her breath she turned for home, hateful Simmins, hiding another secret as dark as their manipulative abilities.

Now she'd have to try to draw the secret from him, and she hated the thought of doing that.

CHAPTER 6

$\mathcal{M}$arc had had a terrible day.

He'd entered the garden through the old Simmins passage, only to be told that 'the king' had left before dawn for the D'argent kingdom. Marc had then been escorted out, and while the guards had been apologetic, they'd also not budged in their duty to obey 'the king.'

Worse, they'd been ordered to make sure he had his birthday gift, the gelada, and as he headed toward the village – as a commoner – his pet trotted after him, pushing its nose into Marc's hand looking for seeds.

Still, Marc comforted himself. He, of course, still had the hearts of the people.

The burgesses were always easy to persuade so

he'd headed into the village, starting with the black-smith. Simple, kind man.

The blacksmith would be easy to convert to his side.

With hopeful heart, Marc entered the darkened smithy's shop, blinking cheerfully despite the blinding heat coming from the hearth.

"Yer – Majesty!" The blacksmith's tongs dropped with a clank as the man stood, looking toward him.

Marc smiled but then realized the man was looking past him.

"That's just a gelada. Do not fear, Burgess Smith. It's ugly, but it's a sweet creature."

The man nodded, staring at the baboon which was crouched at the door by a stale-looking bucket of water, scooping out handfuls with its large hand and bending it's lips back to show its pleasure.

"See?" Marc gestured, swallowing his impatience. "It even likes to smile. It's my pet. I'm calling him Smiles."

"Smiles, a good pet to be sure." The man wouldn't take his eyes from it.

"Yes. Yes. So, do tell people not to be afraid of him."

"Aye – Sire – er – I mean Mister Marc, Your Majesty, sir." The blacksmith winced miserably.

"Yes, about that. Of course, the whole thing has

become quite overblown." Marc reached forward, picking up the man's dropped tongs and holding them back out to him by the handles.

The man grabbed them, but Marc held on an extra second few seconds, his thumb brushing the man's forefinger and feeling quickly.

Strange. Two thoughts struggled within the man. Agreement, complete and passionate – but another feeling overpowered it, indignation, strangely hazy but strong.

Indignation had a way of overpowering other feelings. He'd learned that early when learning to read people, but what did the smith have to be indignant about?

"I *am* a great king." Marc said almost to himself.

"Yes." The smith agreed quickly. "I know you are – were- the best king Terram has ever had."

"So, I've been told many a time – and to let that end – over being a single minute late."

"Almost two minutes, Sire, - er - Mister Simmins."

"Yes. Two. Two mere minutes – and when held to all I've done – the peace, the prosperity."

Sweat had broken out on the smith's forehead, mixing with the ashy grime, and when the man spoke, it was with conviction. "It's just - the king must obey the law. If the king don't care for the law, what are we ruled by?"

Marc stopped. The exact words Thomis had used – except that Thomis had better grammar, of course.

Burgess Smith turned back to his anvil. "It makes me sorrowful, Sire, very much so, and to think that you married so terribly, besides. I'd have thought you'd care for the people 'o Terram more than that, I would've."

"Married terribly?"

"Aye. She's a peculiar one, she is. A bit frightening, e'en. One minute she's there. Another she isn't. And never heard her say more 'n three words together, neither."

"Well, I like to talk enough for both of us, I suppose. Good day, Burgess Smith."

Simple, foolish man. Marc thought as he headed down the street. Smith had always been a fool.

Certes, Marc would do better with the other burgesses.

He was wrong.

Marc went to every council member, and after calming each of them about the gelada and assuring them that Smiles was a sweet creature, Marc found that every council member felt the same of Marc's fall from the throne.

How had *all* their opinions changed in a matter of a day? How was that possible?

And their words – all so similar.

"We must abide by the law, or we have nothing to hold us together."

"Kings must obey the law, or we will not be bound together."

"The law is what binds us. Kings are also under the law."

What had changed their minds so completely?

He also found out that no one in town liked his wife.

In fact, there was more talk in town about him marrying the tanner than about him losing his kingdom.

"Does she ever talk?" A woman asked.

"She's the real silent type, but if anyone could thaw her, it would be you Sire, sir, or m- m- , Sire." The baker said before awkwardly handing Marc a few rolls as if in apology.

"Did you like the cake, Mister- umm Majesty?"

Cake?

Marc remembered he'd ordered a massive birthday cake, 10 layers and taller than himself. He knew it was to have been drawn in on a brightly painted cart at the height of the birthday ball, but with everything else, he hadn't gone into the ball let alone seen the cake.

"Thank you for the cake - and the rolls." He held up the baker's gift.

"And your order for the fall festival cake is still ordered?" The baker said hopefully.

Marc paused, trying to remember

Thomis had thought the birthday cake too ostentatious so Marc had ordered one double the size for the autumn feast. Peace was more important he'd figured, and he had also thought it would be fun to further anger Thomis.

The cake ordered for the autumn feast was 20 layers and as wide as a man was tall. Marc imagined Thomis' nostrils flaring when he had to pay the bill for a cake the size of two horses.

"Yes. Of course the order for the cake still stands."

The baker was a broad red-haired man with freckles, and as his face flushed, his freckles blended with the blush. "Thank you – yer – Mr. Marc, Sire."

Marc walked around the village another hour, watching the villagers gasp and point at Smiles who grinned congenially at them.

Finally, he sat down on a grassy hill, watching the town as Smiles chewed on a long piece of grass beside him.

"Your Majesty!"

No falter halted the man's voice. There was only confidence using the title Marc no longer possessed.

Marc turned to see his old friend, Petir, coming up the road.

Petir clasped Marc's hand in both of his. "Tis a sad day in Terram, Sire."

Marc nodded, his throat closing. "You are the first to call me sire without mumbling and apologizing."

The physician smiled. "You will always be my king e'en though your domain has shrunk."

"My domain is a tannery, Petir! A tannery!"

"And yet it is what has been given you-"

"By a foolish law - and a bunch of fools –"

"Nay, sire! By the One Father. You think He could not have stopped this? Does He not mean this for good?

Marc stilled, but had to push back. He could not feign faith he didn't have.

"I do not see why He would take a faithful servant as I and demote me to this."

His friend looked sad, but his voice was firm. "Do you remember when you traveled with me in D'argent?"

Marc nodded. He'd been fifteen, and the kingdom of D'argent had been a crumbling heap of its former glory. Pain had been everywhere. He still shuddered when he remembered not wanting to touch the people because it had hurt too much to feel their pain.

"When you traveled with me for those weeks, Sire, how big was your domain?"

"It felt small."

"And what did you do?" Petir was no more than twenty-eight, but his face was lined with sorrow.

"I did what I could."

"Aye. We planted hope."

Marc thought back on it as Petir continued. "A single drink to a beggar, a hug for a child, a conversation with a lonely widow. Each opportunity the One Father gave and used."

Marc nodded. He remembered. Those weeks with Petir had changed his life.

Petir's voice was firm. "Seeds planted in hope grow mighty fruit - if the hope is in the right thing."

"Seeds are so small." Marc smiled ruefully

"Because they are." Petir nodded. "But our job is to plant them for the One Father gives the fruit, and His power is not small."

Petir's words shook Marc's pride.

Who was Marc to tell the One Father where he belonged?

But a tannery? Marc shouldn't be in a tannery! He was supposed to save the kingdom!

"I thought I could fulfill the prophecy." The words were out before he could stop them.

Petir cocked his head. "To unite the kingdoms?"

Marc nodded. "I've never told anyone this, but the night Arianna died, I flew with her. As long as we touched, I had the power of the air. I thought that we were the prophesied souls who'd be entwined and unite the kingdoms."

Petir gaped at him, and Marc continued.

"And I just thought that even though she had died, I could still fulfill the prophecy myself."

Marc looked away not wanting to admit the rest.

How many times had he imagined himself on the ruby-crested Thrush throne, the savior of the kingdoms?

It seemed so silly now that his own people had — albeit apologetically – turned against him.

Old wounds had opened in the last day, pushing pain he'd thought healed to the surface, and he found he had to share the memory he'd not shared with anyone before.

Marc stared down at the village. "When my father was on his death bed, he said it was good Arianna had died. He said people on both sides wanted her dead, and she'd have been killed anyway if she'd survived the fire."

His words came more quickly. If he were to confess this to anyone, it would be Petir. "She had cousins who wanted the D'argentian throne, and the people of Terram wanted the line of Thrush destroyed. I think father was trying to comfort me. He knew – *somehow* — that I loved her though I don't think he could have known we were connected, and of all the things he could have said to me when he was dying, he wanted most to assure me of that. He said if she'd lived the people of D'argent would never have submitted to us, and there never would have been peace."

Marc let himself look at his friend, maybe his only friend, trying to make sense of all the sorrow in his own head.

"No one wanted peace back then. D'argent wanted domination. Terram wanted vengeance, but then the war came. You know eventually everyone was so weary of war, and I thought I could fix everything. I thought I *had* fixed everything for the contract is only three months away, but now I fear for my kingdom. Thomis didn't want the contract, and he will likely drive us back into war."

He saw Petir's face harden. The physician feared the same.

Marc shook his head. "And now what? What do I do in a lonely tannery? What does a king do in a tannery?"

Petir's gaze snapped back. "Plant hope in the tannery, Sire."

Hope. There was no hope at that tannery, but it wasn't him that brought the hopelessness.

Hopelessness had been there long before he had.

Did Aria hope in anything? Something told him

she didn't. Even when she'd been marrying a king, she'd barely shown any feeling.

But how foolish to plant hope in a tannery when his kingdom was on the brink of another war!

He shook Petir's hand and walked on, glad for Smiles who trotted after him. The creature's presence kept the villagers back, and he was glad. He didn't want to talk to anyone else as he walked slowly back through the town, passing the governor's mansion as he reached the edge of the last street.

He could be living there this very moment and enjoying the silken sheets of the governor's daughter's bed, their innumerable servants, and a hearty roast.

If he'd known he'd lose all, would he have still married the lowly tanner?

He kept walking, his mind so hazed with thoughts that he didn't realize he'd reached the tannery until he was hit with the putrid smell and found himself standing on the edge of the clearing, looking down at the grassy hill that swept down to drab grey buildings.

Smiles barreled forward, settling in an especially

long patch of grass that almost hid him from view, and Marc could only see the top of his fluffy hair waving with the heads of grass.

Marc stood silently, feeling like he was at a crossroads.

On the one side was his kingdom, given perhaps by the One Father to Thomis who was terrible with people and would probably push it back into war.

On the other side was a grey, smelly tannery.

Where was his calling?

He reached down, plucking up a long strand of grass and letting the seed head fall into his hand.

Why would the One Father reduce him to this? What good would planting hope do here?

He looked down at his hand, calloused by sword practice but rarely work and then tossed the tiny seeds back on the ground.

A king reduced to a tanner? Foolishness!

How could he do anything here?

His vast domain had shrunk from two large kingdoms and tens of thousands of subjects to a smelly little tannery and one mysterious wife.

Aria.

How long had he wanted to marry her? He wasn't even sure. From the moment he'd met her?

Somehow, it felt like he'd wanted to marry her before he'd even met her. Thomis had always been trying to talk him into a political match, but though his brother had taken everything else – this one thing Marc had.

He'd broken free of that headiness he felt when Thomis talked him into something he didn't want.

Aye, he now had a bare income, a house that stunk – but the wife he'd actually wanted.

Thomis had not taken that, and in the soft evening air, Marc felt like a victor.

She was a strange wife by all accounts.

Beautiful – yes.

Hard-working – a thousand times, yes.

Capable – incredibly so – even with her limp.

But how was it she didn't laugh or even really talk?

She was a mystery to be solved.

And if his duty was to her – it was a next step, and the next step was what he was looking for.

She did not love him - yet, but she would. He still had his charm. It didn't seem to be working its usual magic today, but he'd woo her.

He may not be king at the moment – until he could figure out how to remedy his situation – but he knew he still had enough charm to win a woman if he gave it his full effort.

It should be easy enough.

A small form exited the cottage, and Marc spotted his bride.

She was incredibly graceful. From this distance, it almost appeared she wasn't touching the ground, her back straight, as she glided across to the chicken coop at the center of the yard.

A massive barrel of feed sat on the edge of the enclosure far too large for her to lift.

His duty.

Hope gave him eyes to see past his tenuous circumstances and the courage to recognize his calling.

Aye, it was a small calling, but at least he knew it was his next step.

He jogged across the stubbly grass.

His wife stood in the midst of three dozen chickens and hadn't heard him as he came to the fence and stood only feet behind her.

Despite her efforts, the tight bun she always wore had softened sending strands of silky dark hair around her neck and forehead, and the wisps softened further in the evening breeze.

He stood awkwardly for a moment, debating how to let her know he was behind her.

She moved toward the large pail in something that was too graceful to be a step, and Marc saw the container start to tip.

So much of the grain would be spoiled in the dirt!

He jumped the fence and caught it just as it was tipping, and with a great heave, he righted it.

The dark eyes turned on him, her lips open. She blinked, lowering her form. Had she been on tiptoes? Most likely to catch the box though that would have been futile.

"This is far too heavy, Aria. I'll do it."

Arianna doublechecked her feet were on the ground and tried to calm herself.

How much had he seen? She always did her chores using her air powers. It was too painful to walk otherwise, and it was too heavy to lift the grain barrel and move the two caldrons.

And he'd seen her. By a miracle, he thought it had been tipping by accident.

But how had he not seen her fly across the yard?

She stepped back, watching him tip the barrel and fling the grain to the chickens as she tried to decide how to finish the evening chores with him there.

Impossible. She glanced about; she hadn't carried the caldron in with their supper.

She could not risk him seeing her, but to ask him? To admit the need for help?

But she didn't need to ask. Her spoiled, arrogant prince had already jumped out of the enclosure, and strode to the caldron.

"Is this finished?" He called.

"I – er – yes."

He shook off his expensive velvet coat, pushing it around the hot lip of the caldron before carrying it inside.

Arianna limped hurriedly across the yard, flustered.

CHAPTER 7

By the time she'd reached the cottage, the king had found her only two bowls and was looking for a second spoon.

"There is only one." She managed awkwardly.

"I suppose I'll use the ladle." He smiled. "I'll pray."

She gaped, unsure when she'd prayed last. Why pray to a 'Father' who didn't listen?

She sank into the chair, and he pulled up a stool and was reaching for her hand.

She would have protested, but he'd already bowed his head and started praying. His hand closed over hers, and instantly, her panic and frustration dipped into calm peacefulness.

"Thank you, One Father," Marc began.

Arianna was enraptured. Where had this peace come from?

He was still praying, "...for this food and for our duties, for my – wife."

She could curl up and sleep in this peace, fade into it and never wish to leave it.

I'm not afraid, and I'm so – content – and safe!

Nay, she wasn't safe. Nothing had changed from a minute before.

It's the soul connection. It lies.

But how could this be a lie? Could a lie be so kind?

Yes. Lies that pretend kindness are the worst.

She looked up and realized he had finished praying, and she needed to pull her hand away – though she didn't want to.

She dragged it back, and as soon as her hand left his, she was plunged into the icy cold again.

The peace was completely gone.

She reached desperately in her soul, begging the peace back, but it could not be found there so she forced herself to focus on the king.

He had dished up the soup and then taken two large rolls out of his coat pockets before setting them on the table beside the soup. Finally, he sipped a bit of the soup off the ladle.

His nose crinkled only slightly before he forced his face to neutralize.

She knew that she didn't want to eat the soup so she took a bite of the roll watching him continue on his soup with perfect poise before a movement outside caught her eye.

Something had scooted to the open door, and an ugly little face poked around the edge of the door frame.

A gelada.

She'd been only five the last time she'd seen one, and seeing it now felt almost as absurd as sitting with the king of Terram as he cheerfully drank her horrible-tasting soup from a ladle.

She stared at the animal.

How had a gelada come to Terram?

Its earnest little face poked in farther before it sat back on its haunches.

She looked away from it, trying to block out the memory of the last time she'd seen a gelada. She'd learned she could block bad memories behind the magical wall, but this memory would not be contained, and it hit her fully.

She was five years old again, sitting in her beautiful little silver throne beside her father's huge ruby and gold throne.

It was one of her father's lavish parties, and she'd

been allowed to stay up and watch. It was late though. The hours of watching the feasters and minstrels had run together, and she had been starting to nod off.

Suddenly, the steward of the feast had announced a monster from the Jade Isles.

At the time, she'd not known much of the Jade Isles. They only sounded mysterious and exciting, and she'd instantly waked.

The gelada had been brought in within a gold cage, and the steward had made a show of setting the cage in the open space before the high table.

She'd sat as straight as she could, trying to appear brave despite it's ugliness – but then her father had ordered it to be dragged out of the cage.

"Please don't, Father!" She'd begged. "It's a monster!"

"Never show fear, Arianna." he'd reprimanded. "You are a Thrush, fearless and strong. Act it."

But the creature had not been a mean monster. It had been afraid, crawling under a table and trying to hide until the guards had dragged it out and another animal was brought in, a snapping, hissing badger on a chain, and before Arianna realized it, they'd thrust the badger into the cage with the gelada.

"Fight! Fight!" The guests had cheered.

But it really was no fight. The gelada shrieked and tried to escape, but it did not last long.

She'd held the tears back, trying to show her father she was brave, and when it was over, and the animal's remains had been carried out, she had sat still, unable to speak or eat – and holding the sadness inside.

Marc Simmins stood, his movement bringing her back to the present.

He stepped toward the door, his hands outstretched. "It won't hurt you. Do not be afraid of it."

Afraid?

"Who would be afraid of a gelada?" she snapped

"You know what it is?" His jaw dropped. "I've been all over the town, and everyone was terrified of it."

"Only a fool would be afraid of a gelada." She stood, tossing the contents of her untouched soup bowl back into the caldron before looking back at him.

His perplexed face turned to the caldron.

Maybe he was wondering if she poisoned it. *Good.*

"I'll wash out the dishes," he snapped briskly.

"There is a creek down the hill," she replied, eyeing the huge vat and debating how to clean up the untouched soup.

It was a long walk though she'd always used her powers to carry the water back and forth. How could she manage to drag everything down with her limp? Surely, he'd be of no help.

She was wrong again. Marc Simmins threw the dishes into the still-full caldron and was out the door, the bitter stew sloshing across the yard as he carried it.

Arianna straightened the already-neat cottage, unsure what had happened – nor what would happen when he came back. The last of the sunlight was gone, and she lit a single candle, still confused by the change in the spoiled king.

She'd expected him to continue his pouting, but Marc Simmins had changed from the night before.

He was back sooner then she'd expected, and all the dishes were clean, including the empty caldron.

She stood awkwardly as he set them down, a smile playing at his lips. "The soup was terrible."

"Aye," she agreed, deciding to sit at the table since she was unsure of what else to do.

His smiled broadened. "I am sorry for my lack of manners this morning. It was unfitting for the morning after our weddding."

"Aye." She folded her hands on the table and then tried them in her lap. Both places felt awkward.

She did not want any apology, never from a Simmins.

He slid onto the stool and in one smooth motion

tweaked her nose playfully in a gesture an older brother might do.

She forgot her hands altogether.

He was still grinning. "So, every time I am a knave, do you plan to make inedible food?"

She could feel her face heat.

"I – well —"

"But you forgot that then you also would have nothing to eat then either. 'Tis a good thing the baker likes me."

"The whole of Terram likes you." Her voice sounded bitter even to her ears.

He cocked his head, his face growing serious. "True – except maybe one young woman; her regard I must earn."

Arianna could not breathe, and without realizing, she'd reached one hand up on the table.

Automatically, he did what she'd not realized she'd hoped he'd do, and he grabbed her hand. The happiness of the soul connection filled her instantly.

His beautifully impish smile had returned. "Soon, *everyone* will like me."

It was a promise. He would win her, and with the warmth bubbling through her like a fountain as his lips brushed the back of her calloused hand, she almost thought he could keep it.

But he couldn't –

She looked past him to the hearth. Under one of the stones, she'd hidden the pin he'd given her thirteen years earlier. She'd started to love him that night, the seemingly sweet boy who'd pretended to care.

She could not do that again.

Marc glanced back to where his wife was staring. Was she looking at the fire? No, just to the right of it though there was nothing there.

He looked back, and she'd closed her eyes, her delicate brows pulled down in concentration.

With her eyes closed, she reminded him again of the girl he'd flown with as a child.

Everything was the same, the porcelain-like face, the perfect nose, the lip shape with the fuller lower lip -

But then she opened her eyes, and their depths drowned him again.

Tumultuous, dark – and frightening in a thrilling, curious way. Those dark, turbulent eyes were the opposite of the placid face.

Nay. She could not be Arianna. This woman was that girl's opposite.

She jerked her hand back quickly, rising and smoothing her palms down her skirt.

"It is late, and there is much work to be done tomorrow." She said brusquely.

Marc nodded, starting to stand. He'd expected to woo her better, and he tried to think where he'd gone wrong.

He stepped back and tripped over something. It was a poor, make-shift bed in the corner of the cottage. A few armloads of what felt like straw barely held the thin blanket off the stone floor.

Marc went cold. This was where his wife had slept the night before; he'd taken the only bed.

"Oh, forgive me Aria!" He stared at her, taking in her widened eyes. "I really am a hedge-born fool!"

She shook her head furiously. "You are a king –

"I am first a husband."

She didn't seem to understand what he meant so Marc explained. "I should take that." He pointed toward the corner, grabbing her hand to pull her toward the wall. He had guessed it would take his wife time before they shared a bed though it seemed it would also take time before she'd even talk to him more than a few words.

Color rushed into the pale cheeks, and she fisted her hands.

Her words came out slowly. "I – don't need your – *pity*."

Was that it?

"Because of your limp?" He had to fight to stay calm. The townspeople had not been wrong. She was ridiculous. "It's not pity. It's because you have value."

"I didn't ask you to value me," she snapped.

"I swore it in my vows!" He pushed his hand through his hair.

"But I didn't – " She broke off.

"In my vows, I swore to value you, and my sin would be against the One Father if I broke my vow to Him."

She was still staring at him so Marc decided to make his point completely clear, and scooping her up, he perched her on the bed and stepped back with finality.

She sat, staring at him, her black eyes ginormous, and unblinking until Marc felt awkward.

"Do you forgive me for my rudeness this morning?" he asked.

She looked down at her hands, ignoring his question. "I do not need this. I do not know why you are being kind, but I don't need or want anything from you."

ARIANNA KEPT her face looking away until Marc Simmins turned, running his fingers through his wavy hair for the second time and walked toward the "bed" she'd made the night before in the corner.

Silently, she lay down and watched him blow out the candle before trying to fluff the bit of straw with jerky movements.

It had been ten years since her eyes had warmed with tears, but now, Arianna was blinking furiously, thankful for the dark.

He'd given her the better bed.

She had been grateful for his complaining, but kindness?

She hated that.

Marc Simmins flopped down on the make-shift bed which was a mistake. She heard his head smash against the stone floor and heard his muffled groan.

Why had he been so congenial? How had he not pressured her to give him his marital rights?

"Are you sleeping?" he asked suddenly.

She winced. Now he would pressure her.

"I wish to be," she snapped, "but now I am awake."

"I was curious as to where you'd seen a gelada before."

"In a fight. It was made to fight a badger."

His voice opened with shock. "It could not do that! What wicked knave would make it do such a thing?"

Wicked?

Anger heated her instantly. How dare a Simmins call her father wicked! It was not her father who was wicked – it was the Simmins – and Marc Simmins – the cocky king who lay on the floor of her cottage *pretending* he wanted to be there.

Part of her wished to leap from the bed and tell him he was wrong, but instead, she did what she always did; she gathered all her anger toward him and used it to fuel her hatred, strengthening her wall. She needed it secure.

And then with as much calm as she could muster, she answered. "People do foolish things. I am tired. Let us sleep."

But Marc Simmins was not the kind of husband who could be told to go to sleep, and rather than listen, he sat up, his voice filled with conviction.

"Aria, it was not foolish to kill the gelada. Do not reduce it to foolishness. Killing for sport is wicked, and the people who did it were wicked. One thing I learned as king was to call wickedness what it is and never make excuses for it."

Aria bit her lip so hard she could taste blood. It was Marc Simmins, a thieving, murdering Simmins who was wicked! And she was the strong Thrush who was brave – and – good.

"You disagree they were wicked?" he demanded, stoking the fire he didn't know burned.

"No! Er – yes!"

"You disagree?" The horror in his voice twisted her in two.

"It wasn't as simple as that." She tried to explain, running back in her mind what had always driven her father. "There needed to be a show of strength."

Yes. Her father had always wished to showcase his power, and shows of strength were frequent.

"A show of strength? 'Twas a clear show of weakness."

"The man was not weak!"

"Of a surety he was. His actions showed he was a bully!"

Bully? Aria didn't move. Her father, a bully? Nay.

Her "husband" was still talking. "Smiles would be afraid of his own reflection!" He paused. "Though maybe there would be some reason for that."

"Are you ever silent?" Arianna hissed.

"When I'm sleeping."

"Then sleep!"

"First, answer me, for now I want to know what you think. Do you or do you not think the man was wicked to do such a thing?"

How had she married such a stubborn wretch? Hateful soul curse!

She swallowed and then swallowed again, remembering back to the laughter and lude yells, admitting what she'd never let herself see before.

"Yes."

"Yes?"

"Yes. They – he – was wicked! There, you won!"

He started, and she feared he would stand. "I was not trying to win, Aria. I simply wanted to know your opinion. It seemed you were defending him."

"I was not. I – I just did not understand."

She rolled over, hoping he would cease speaking, and he finally did.

And as his breathing slowed, she felt her own anger growing.

How dare he speak to her of wickedness when e'en now Casimir rotted in his dungeon. If it weren't for Marc's rash marriage proposal, Casimir would be free.

And now, because of Marc's delay, he was not king and she was not queen so she could free Casimir. How was she to get him out?

The only way to save him was to break him out, and 'twas clear she'd have to do it.

But how? The door did not open.

By day, it would be impossible so she'd have to go by night. That meant her only option would be to fly over the wall, but at least two guards patrolled the upper walk around the castle.

Did she dare?

She knew from the rebel reports that they carried crossbows. She'd be fully exposed in the air, and if they saw her, she'd never be able to fly away fast enough.

But how many times did Casimir save me? She thought.

How many times had Casimir stood up to leering watchers when they were still children and Arianna was a dancer, daily displayed and constantly vulnerable?

And when she'd been crippled and had to stay in Terram, Casimir had stayed as well.

Their friendship had grown, and their hearts had been joined in one goal: to bring down the Simmins and avenge D'argent. But he had stayed while the gypsies had gone back to Vacilocha, and he'd watched out for Arianna.

Aye. There was no choice. She needed to free him. Mayhap, Marc Simmins would have been gentle with a hot-headed rebel, but no-doubt Thomis would see the real risk Casimir was.

The anger and fear twisted together until Aria was numb with them, and when she was sure Marc slept, she silently donned her pitch-black cloak and slipped out of the cottage flying fast and high in the night sky.

CHAPTER 8

The castle came into view like a black light-studded box far beneath. She lowered slowly, hoping that the cloudy night would make her look like a shadow to untrained eyes.

But the darkness worked against her as well for it was impossible to see where the night watchmen walked, and each carried a crossbow.

The soldiers of Terram had always been known for their strength with the cross bow, the one thing that her people had been weaker on.

One shot would be all that it would take, and she'd fall like a wounded bird – several hundred feet.

She was almost to the wall now, and there had been no yells from below. The guards must be on the other end of wall.

Arriana landed quickly on the upper walkway and slid down the wall, heart throbbing. It would never have worked if it the night had not been cloudy, but with the moonlight covered and mayhap a bit of celestial help she'd made it within the wall.

Of course, now came the worst part. She'd have to make it into the belly of the castle and down into the dungeon.

Staying close against the wall, she pushed the air silently around herself, floating a hand's breadth from the walk and listening for the tread of soldier's boots. 'Twas obvious the Terramites were not afraid of attack. Only a guard or two paced the castle on each level, and Arianna avoided them easily, slipping down one corridor and on to another with her dark cape pulled tightly around herself. Years of memorizing the layout of the castle from conversations and crude maps Casimir had drawn aided her now, and ten minutes later, she'd made it down to the dungeon which also was unguarded.

For a dungeon, the place was clean, and the cells were open – save one.

The key hung on a peg by the wall, and Arianna grabbed it.

By the time she'd opened the lock and pushed the door open, Casimir was standing, blinking at her in the darkness.

"Aria?" He gaped. "How –

"You know I'm the only one who can get past." she whispered, looking around his cell for any of his possessions. Nothing.

He strode past her, checking around the corner. "What does your husband think of this exploit?"

She heated but shook her head. "There were at least four guards on the main floor, four on the wall, but I think only two out in the courtyard."

He grabbed a rope hanging on the wall beside several other tools. "Through the courtyard then. If we can cross it, the outer wall is short. We can climb it using this."

His eyes lowered to her feet. "I'll help you climb when we get there."

She nodded, knowing she didn't need help and followed him quickly up the stairs, floating, her long skirt brushing the ground and covering her suspended feet.

At the top of the stairs, they paused on a landing where one set of stairs ascended to the tower and another diverged into a hall.

They'd need to slip through the inner hall which led to the outer courtyard, but Casimir paused, looking at the torch at the wall.

She wished he would not. They needed stealth though she knew he wanted the weapon, but thankfully, he knew better than to reach for the torch and stepped into the hall.

She could hear no one. They only had to make it to the end – and then they'd have a chance.

One more corridor, the longest. If the night watch came down while they were in the middle, they'd be seen, but if by pure chance they could make it down quickly enough, they'd make the back staircase entrance and out to the courtyard.

"How are you not limping?" He paused at the corner, checking around it.

Arianna tried to think of a lie. "I – I – do you want me to limp?"

His mouth tipped as he raced down the hall. "No. But I look forward to your explanation after we escape."

They reached the very middle when footsteps sounded ahead.

She froze. There was no time, and she watched in horror as two guards rounded the corner,

Casimir jumped in front of her, and reached for the single flaming torch that hung on the wall.

What would a torch be against two swords?

Sure, that she was hidden behind Casimir, Arianna, reached around him, pushing the air toward the guards and knocking them backwards.

The hall was left in pitch blackness as the torch was extinguished.

"You!" Casimir gasped, groping until he had a hold of her. "You – did – you -?"

Shouts from beyond the hall stopped him mid-sentence, and he pushed her back in the direction they'd come. There would be no stealth now.

"Back!" She gasped. "To the stair. We could go up -"

She flew easily, speeding faster than him up to the second floor, but the yelling had increased. The whole castle was waking!

"The tower. I came down this way!" She shot down the hall toward the opening that led to the upper walkway.

Casimir dashed behind her though she feared she led him wrong. Already, the night watch on the wall would have heard the shouts.

But then they'd made it up the stairs and had darted out into the upper walk, standing on the walkway that circled the top of the castle.

They stood for several seconds, looking for an escape, but guards could be heard hollering from below, and down the wall, someone responded.

They'd have only seconds before the night watch reached them.

"You have to jump," she gasped. "I can aid you from behind."

Casimir pushed her in front of him. "I'll not jump first, leaving you here."

The yells were on the stairs now, Arianna twisted out if his grasp. "I have the power of Thrush, Casimir. I can fly. You must jump first so I can break your fall. Then I'll rise straight up instead of down. It will be safer for me. Now go!"

Reluctantly, he nodded and reaching back into the corridor, he lifted a torch high into the air as he stepped to the edge of the wall.

"I'll draw their arrows. They will see the light and aim for me. You can fly?"

No surprise, only urgency in his voice.

"I – I can. Yes. I fly."

Without a second glance, he jumped, and Arianna raced to the edge, ignoring the yells from behind as she pushed the air under him and pushed him up, up – over the outer wall and farther –

Her arms ached, and she didn't hear the thud of boots behind her until she realized she only had seconds before they would see her.

She had to jump now!

But how could she fly and stop him from falling?

How could she divide her powers?

She didn't know how, and as she leapt; she fo-

140

cused her attention on Casimir on the other side of the field even as she careened toward the ground.

Finally, she shot one final gust to stop his fall and then, at the last second, she started to pull up, but she'd misjudged, and her bad leg hit the ground full-force with an all-to familiar crack.

No.

She struggled up, yells closing in from behind. Should she fly back up? Around her arrows were shooting fast, one nearly missing her, but as she looked, she realized they weren't shooting at her – but at the edge of the wood toward the torch that Casimir was waving like a fool, risking his neck as if she hadn't just saved it.

She started to fly toward Casimir, pain making her dizzy.

"Fly away!" she heard Casimir shout through the fog.

Hazy with pain, she soared straight up into the air, her black cloak making her invisible in the night sky.

The pain was so bad that she could barely think, and she struggled to stay conscious as she flew.

Finally, her cottage came into view, and she soared toward it.

Almost – almost inside –

She zipped straight toward the door, but as she

landed, her bad leg buckled, and she hit the threshold, crumpling into a ball until the pain made everything fade to black.

Men's voices brought Arianna back into consciousness.

As her vision cleared, Arianna realized she was on the bed in the cottage, and there, towering above Marc Simmins, stood a broad man with incredible posture and a disciplined stride.

Arianna's heart lurched. The stranger was clearly a soldier.

Had she been seen after all? Had they come to take her?

She tried to think how to escape, but Marc Simmins and the soldier were standing between her and the closed door.

Her "husband" turned, seeing she'd woken, and he dropped to one knee beside the bed. "What happened, Aria?"

Only concern lined his tone. No accusation. Was it possible he did not suspect anything?

Hopeful, she groped for any possible story.

"I - slipped. The gelada - was on the roof. I was trying to get him down. I feared he'd break through the roof."

The soldier was frowning. "You fell with great force."

Marc Simmins took her hand, and her heart pounded harder, making her leg throb.

"This is Petir, Aria." He said. "Petir is a physician, and he can set your leg."

Petir the physician.

Arianna had heard of this man. Some had called him an angel, and there had been many stories of his aid around D'argent during the war, as well as rumors he was in league with the famous and mysterious Laelynn, but as Arianna stared at him, she saw he was just a man, mayhap five or ten years older than herself.

"When you fell the last time, did a true physician set your leg?" Petir asked.

Arianna shook her head slowly. Money had been tight, and the head gypsy had called in an old woman who had claimed to know what she was doing and would do it for a good price.

Petir nodded. "This is of the One Father then for it is a very good break."

"There is such thing as a good break?" she asked, frustrated that she couldn't seem to let go of Marc

Simmin's hand. She was likely cutting off the circulation to his fingers.

"I could not have done it better," the physician explained. "It rebroke in the same place, but I think I can bind it so it heals correctly this time."

What did he mean, 'heals correctly?'

Warmth shot up her arm from where she held his hand, and her heart skipped even though her mind still struggled to understand what they were saying. It had healed before –

And suddenly, she realized what they meant though Marc Simmins expressed it first. "She could walk without a limp?"

"Less of one. Of that, I am certain, Sire. Likely, she will fully heal, and she'll be able to walk with no limp at all."

Fully heal. The soft words reverberated around her like the lapping of water in a warm pool.

Fully heal. Fully heal.

She closed her eyes, too frightened to hope. It couldn't be true.

Marc Simmins and the physician started laying out utensils and bandages on the table, and their tones were light and cheerful as they worked.

It was curious to see this side of Marc Simmins. He was not a king or an enemy. He was this physician's friend and a rather normal person.

She didn't like seeing him as anything but a Sim-mins, but it was too late.

"'Tis good I had stopped to bid you farewell." Petir said to this normal Marc.

"How long since you've been back to your vil-lage?" Marc asked.

"Twelve years. I plan to buy a huge flock of sheep, settle in my village and have ten children."

"And if the peace doesn't hold?" Marc's voice strained, and Arianna listened carefully. Was the peace treaty not as definite as was believed?

"If war comes again, you'll have my aid, sire."

Marc considered this several seconds.

"Will you come to the autumn ball?" he asked, "It will be good to have allies there for the signing of the treaty."

"I'll be back for the autumn ball." The physician promised, and the firmness in his tone told her there was indeed more than they were saying.

She watched as Marc laid out the several strips of white cloth, and Petir chuckled. "You remembered exactly what I need. Do you remember how to wrap a bandage?"

"I remember." Marc said evenly, "But we are missing cold water for a compress to take down the swelling when we are finished setting the bone." He looked toward her, his gaze nauseatingly sympathetic, and Arianna shifted. When they set the bone, the pain would be excruciating, and Marc Simmins would witness her at her weakest.

Certes, she would not scream or weep. She'd not cried since the night Marc betrayed her, but what if she groaned like a babe or writhed like a dog? She'd hate for him to see that.

"I'll get the hot water." Marc announced heading out of the cottage with a bucket.

Arianna watched the physician measure some liquid into the spoon before handing it to her. "This is for the pain. As soon as your husband returns, we will set the bone."

He gently laid his hands along her shin, pushing slightly.

She wished he'd stop, but she grit her teeth and asked, "Could you set it now? I do not wish to wait!"

The physician paused. The man had wise brown eyes, and they bore into her for several seconds before he saw something that caused him to nod. "Very well."

She closed her eyes, steeling herself for the pain until she felt ready.

She was wrong.

It was worse than the break, for somehow, he'd taken ahold of both bones and pushed them together.

She sucked in hard fighting the desire to twist away as the bones ground together, and she felt as if she were being pelted and bruised all over her body. Was she hallucinating?

The pain was too bad to open her eyes, but through the haze, she knew he was wrapping the ankle.

The minute felt like a year, but Arianna swallowed the shriek. She'd not scream, and she sucked harder which caused the bruising around the rest of her body to worsen.

Finally, his hands pulled back, and she opened her eyes.

The physician stood beside her, his shocked face eye level with hers though a minute earlier his height had made him tower above her.

Arianna blinked and then realized the horrible truth. In her pain, she'd risen into the air above the tall doctor's head, sucking the air and a few dozen objects in around her and throwing wind around the cottage in what must have been like a whirlwind.

Only his reflexes had allowed him to still wrap the ankle.

Hurriedly, she dropped herself back on to the bed staring at his shocked face.

"You are of the house of Thrush." He gasped. "I thought they were all dead."

"Because your people killed them!" she spat, sweat making her shiver with rage – and terror.

"They killed each other. After King Thrush died, they fought within themselves."

He backed up, and then his eyes opened in realization. "You are Arianna Thrush! That's why Marc chose you! You are the fulfillment of the prophecy!"

She'd planned to deny that she was the queen, but now she froze.

"What prophecy?"

"You don't know?"

At her silence he swung his hand around emphatically. "*The* prophecy! The one that every child of Terram took heart in for the last hundred years, and the one that was meant to bring peace and prosperity to all our lands! He cleared his throat. "'Once every thousand years, two souls are entwined, uniting the powers of the kingdoms.' You and Marc are the answer to the prophecy!"

"No. We aren't," she whispered.

"You share powers when you touch?"

"He can fly," she admitted, looking up.

"You are the souls prophesied. Your joining has been planned by the One Father and was prophesied over a thousand years ago."

Arianna was stunned. All this time she'd thought the soul connection had been her fault, but if there really were a prophecy, it was just another stroke against her from the One Father and the Simmins family. Not only had her kingdom been stolen, she'd been tied before birth to her enemy – and her fate.

The physician took a step toward the door, and she realized he was going to find Marc.

"Wait!" Arianna gasped desperately. Could she persuade him to keep her secret?

She knew of this man's character. He was a hero of her people even though he was a Terramite. If any one citizen of Terram would be her ally, it would be him.

She took a deep breath and did something she'd never thought she'd ever do: she begged.

"I implore you. If you have any mercy in your heart, do not tell the king my true identity."

"What?" He turned; his face instantly hard.

"Please, if you care for my people even a little, and if you wish for peace as you claim, do not tell him. He will pit the D'argentian throne against the Terramite one trying reclaim power!"

"He is not so wicked!" the physician ground. "You do not know him at all!"

Despite her pain, she forced herself to sit up. "Aye. I know him! He betrayed me once on the night my people were slain. He'll do it again to get what he wants, and you are wrong to think he'll not!"

He scoffed. "He would never! He's a good man."

Over the physician's shoulder, Arianna saw Marc break the tree line. She'd failed. In seconds, Marc would know.

Deep inside her, the anger found a voice, and she spoke in a hiss.

"Marc Simmins feigns love, but it's not real. He's as proud as all the Simmins. He's too proud for a peasant wife and a drab tannery, and no soul curse will keep him from abandoning me!"

The physician's face softened. "How blind your hate makes you, my lady," he murmured, his voice lined with sympathy.

Marc's whistling outside announced his coming, and Arianna had barely settled back on the bed before he popped through the door.

"Petir," he announced, holding up a sloshing bucket. "You were right. This is my call."

The physician turned as Marc was staring around the cottage.

"What happened in here?" Marc asked.

"The gelada came in," Arianna lied quickly.

The physician was frowning. "Your wife –"

"-needs my help! I know exactly what I must do now. I must help her heal. Isn't it amazing I already know so much about tending the sick? It was clearly the One Father preparing me."

The physician tried again. "But the prophecy, Sire- "

Marc snapped his head up. "Who was I to tell the One Father how to save the kingdoms? Who was I to think I could manipulate the prophecy? Nay. *My job is here.* I'm going to win my wife's heart." He pointed toward Aria and then winked at her.

The wink was so out of place, Aria might have laughed if she were not paralyzed with fear. As soon as Marc stopped blathering on, the physician would speak!

The physician shook his head in frustration. "My lord, I need to speak with you about your wife. She's not – not what she appears. She is -"

Marc turned to him, his face serious and his tone that of a king.

"I know. No one understands why I married her. Do not start with me, friend. Isn't it enough to know this is my calling now? You were right, Petir. I see it clearly now. *This* is where I must plant seeds of hope!"

Marc began picking items up and setting them on

shelves, and Arianna watched the physician's face press into decision.

She bit her lip. This was a man of action. She could see it in the way he walked and held himself. He'd not let Marc interrupt him this time.

Aria held her breath as the man strode over to her husband so Marc had to stop and face him.

"Sire," The physician looked past Marc, meeting Arianna's gaze. "I set her leg, and she's – going to be alright. I think she will even walk without a limp, but you must keep her leg bandaged as I taught you. Do you remember?

"Of course." Marc was glowing.

The physician had kept her secret.

"And the medicine? Do you remember the amounts?" Petir asked.

"Yes." Marc replied, pushing little bottles around on the table. "Two parts of this to one part of that, and a half part of that. It will keep the swelling down as well as the pain."

The physician nodded. "Then I'll leave you to tend her, Sire, but- do not –" He paused, his face still conflicted. "Do not forget to plant hope."

"Of course!" Marc laughed. "I told you that is what I intend to do."

Marc was whistling and straightening the cottage as the physician knelt beside Arianna's bed, checking her bandage one last time. His voice was so low, Arianna knew Marc could not hear. "You're wrong about him, my queen, but I'll let him prove it to you."

Arianna opened her mouth to disagree when she realized what the physician had called her.

He looked at her long and hard before standing and turning to Marc and bidding him good bye.

And then with a decisive step, the physician marched through the door without looking back, and she was alone in the cottage with Marc who was busy straightening.

Dumbfounded, she stared at the open doorway.

Why had he kept her secret?

Could it be, the foolish physician had thought Marc would win her?

Of course, he was wrong. Marc's father had taken her kingdom, and Marc– he'd done things too. What were they again?

He was proud. Yes, the man who was organizing her little cottage was – so proud. And cocky, so cocky, but his cockiness was rather endearing and charming now…

But also, he was foolishly optimistic.

There were no seeds that could grow here.

She smoothed her hands over her hair, trying to push the many dissenting strands back into the bun.

"You do not need to do this."

He stopped, and she regretted having caught his attention.

He strode over to the bed and grabbed her hand, kissing the knuckles so charmingly she missed for several seconds that he was trying to read her.

"Wait, he whispered. "It's – it's there somewhere. No –"

She jerked her hand out.

He stood, a curious expression screwing his lips into a boyish smile. "Are you a bit magic, Aria?"

"No more than you."

He chuckled and grabbed a piece of leather. "Teach me how to scrape it."

"Why?"

"How else will we eat but through leather craft?"

"But – you are no tanner!"

His face clouded for a fraction of a breath but then broke into a smile again.

"For now, I am, and I will plant here while I'm a tanner."

"Plant?" She took the knife, scraping down the skin and wishing she'd done it the day before.

"Aye. Give me three months, Aria, and you'll see something growing from it. Besides, now that I am a tanner, that is one of the many things you and I have in common."

"Methinks, we have nothing in common." The

pain liquid from the physician was taking hold, and she felt her head clearing.

"Well, we are both people of Terram."

"Yes." *No,* she corrected in her head.

"And we both want peace," Marc added.

"Yes." *No.*

"We both are good dancers."

"I cannot dance anymore."

"You will. In three months when your leg is fully healed.

She stilled, trying to imagine dancing again, to feel the air twirling around her and the joy of being one with it –

Nay, surely, the doctor had been wrong.

"Do not hope in an impossible goal." she whispered.

"Hope gives you the courage to see your goals." He rose, holding up the fully-scraped leather. "What do we put on it now?"

She stared, trying to think how he'd finished so quickly. "Next we boil that one, but over there is a different skin that needs to be rubbed with the paste in that jar."

He grabbed the jar, opened it, and grimaced, choking back several coughs as he lay the skin on the table.

"So, what do you like about being a tanner?" he

asked, his voice husky.

"The quiet."

He chuckled. "That will not last."

"It's already gotten much louder the last two days."

"And it will be louder still. One of the gifts to the Simmins is we have twins."

Twins.

Arianna tried to imagine keeping two flying babies a secret. It would be impossible. Her identity would be discovered immediately.

Marc looked up "I loved having a twin brother. Did you have sisters or brothers?"

"No. I was alone."

Alone. Always alone.

He saw her tense and came over to her again, his voice lowering as he took her hands. "And now you are not. That is another thing we have in common. Neither of us is alone."

"I liked being alone," Arianna murmured as she leaned forward.

"Mayhap, you thought you liked it. Certes, you were used to it." His eyes had dropped to her lips, and he was leaning forward.

Did he mean to kiss her?

"I'm not ready!" She scooted back.

He nodded, blinking out of his daze.

"Of course. I'll give you time." He strode back to the table. "And I'll be sleeping on the floor bed for now. Take the time you need, Aria."

He went back to smearing the paste, his voice cheerful again, "So, it seems we have much in common. We are both future parents of twins, we are both owners of the only gelada in Terram, and – "

He paused meaningfully, "In three months, Aria, you and I will both be happy together.

She shrugged. "Maybe."

Never.

CHAPTER 9

MONTH ONE

*L*aundry.

It had been 4 sennights, a whole month, and the chores were endless.

Marc waded into the ice-cold brook, thrusting the soiled shirt down into the water.

The water blackened from the pitch-black soap, and he rubbed his hands over the fabric until his fingers had lost their feeling.

Tossing the blanket over a high branch, he paused to watch the early morning sun crystalize the waterdroplets.

His wife still ignored him, his kingdom was racing to ruin, and he was too buried in chores to do a single thing about it all.

Stripped of everything else, all he had left were chores.

He grabbed a shirt and smashed the soap into it, forcing his numb hands under the icy water again.

Never a thanks - only cold gazes from expressionless dark eyes.

Here he was, the servant of the One Father Himself, sent to her bedside!

How could she remain as stone?

Arianna held back from the cottage doorway so that she would not cast a shadow and alert Marc of her presence.

Marc was making her bed!

Her leg had hurt more than she'd expected the past weeks, and, not wanting to risk it healing badly, she'd let Marc do all the work, awed again and again by his cheerfulness and tenderness.

Of course, she told herself it was the least he could do. He had no other option than to learn to be a tanner.

But why the cheerfulness?

And now, he had gone beyond, determining what extra needs she might have?

E'en at this moment, he was making the bed with clean bedding and humming.

Humming!

She'd wanted to wash her bedding, but with Marc there, she couldn't risk flying to the creek.

Marc pushed the soft, clean blanket around her bed, and Arianna slid back from the door, thankful he'd not seen her.

She wished he'd been cruel. She'd needed him to be.

Cruelty could have strengthened her protection wall and grown a hundred more roots, justifying her plan to destroy his family and avenge hers, but he'd been foolishly kind – steady in his tireless attempts to "plant hope."

Frustrated that she'd come to crave the feeling of the soul connection, she marched into the cottage, grabbing his hand away from the blanket and letting out a quick breath at the wave of happiness that always accompanied his touch.

"I meant to do that," she mumbled, letting the feelings envelope her.

He paused, blips pulsing through the warmth as he turned.

The warmth ignited, heating her until she

thought she'd burst, and as she looked into his face, she realized her own happiness was in sync with his broad smile.

She swallowed, letting go, and was instantly dropped back into the cold. Without meaning to, she shivered.

Marc grabbed a blanket from the end of the bed and tucked it firmly around her shoulders before heading back out the door.

Arianna stared at the empty doorway, realizing for the first time what the feelings had been.

I can read his feelings.

Just like he took on the power of the air when they touched, she could take on the Simmins' power to read others' emotions.

All this time, she thought she was just feeling the magic of the soul connection, but she'd really been reading *him.*

And while the protection spell stopped him from reading her, she'd been able to feel everything he felt.

The warmth was his happiness.

It had been so long since she'd felt happy, she'd forgotten what it felt like.

But what was more, it felt as if the powerful magic that filled her was the opposite of happiness.

But did she not have every right to be unhappy? Was she not the one who had been stolen from?

Aye, she was the victim.

Voices outside interrupted her thoughts, and Arianna saw the woodcarver and a few of his children outside.

Smiles was racing toward them, smiling amiably, and the woodcarver's children were shrieking and scrambling up on the fence.

"Don't fear him! He's smiling at you!" Marc was yelling as he dashed toward them.

Arianna slid to the side of the door, eager to avoid curious stares.

One month ago, weeks could go by without any visitor but Casimir. Now, villagers came daily, joking about the smell and glancing nervously about for a glimpse of the "monster" but coming nonetheless.

At first, they'd claimed to come because they'd heard about her fall and wished to bring something, but mostly, they seemed to want to talk to Marc, often staying nary unto an hour chatting with him about town issues he no longer had authority to do anything about and usually bringing an offering of food because they all said they knew he "could not cook."

Arianna stood silently, straining to hear. Of course, she listened to pass on information to the rebels though despite having learned much the last weeks from eavesdropping, she'd never made it over to the rebel camp.

Marc was uncannily good with the people who betrayed him, and despite all, Arianna could not help respect him as a leader. If the rebels didn't strike soon, Marc may indeed win back his crown by sheer charm.

Half an hour later, Marc was calling his goodbyes through the open door while dumping an armload on the table.

"I'd asked Tobies to carve me two more bowls."

"Why?" she demanded.

"So, we can invite people in to eat with us, and now we could have four visitors, for his two young sons each wanted to make us something, and now we have six! Aren't they nice?" He held up two poorly carved bowls that were roughly the same size as the rest.

"No."

He chuckled and held up two folded pies that smelled of ground meat and spices. "And his wife sent pasties."

Arianna limped to the table as an idea came to her.

Years ago, he had used his power to read her emotions. Why could she not now do the same?

Reaching forward, Arianna grabbed the bowl Marc still held and slid her fingers over his.

"Is it strange to accept charity?" she asked.

Instantly, she felt him heat. *Anger.* Yes, despite his smiles and determined happiness, he was indeed still proud.

"They are gifts." he said, but the heat she felt in him didn't match his words.

"Does it bother you that you are reduced to needing them?" she pressed.

The heat rose, but as quickly, a force of calm overpowered the heat.

"My people love me." He pulled away from her, setting a pasty on each of their places.

"They are not your people anymore."

"They will always be my people."

"But you are not their king. Your kingdom was stolen; you were betrayed. You still call them your people?"

He sighed, pushing his hand through his hair before lining up the bowls up on the shelf; then he lined them up two more ways, his back to her and his shoulders tight.

Swinging back suddenly, he held out a bowl.

"A bowl can be used to serve the king's soup, or it can sit on the floor in the kitchen and hold slop for the pigs. It is still a bowl. Its station is reduced, but its purpose is the same."

"'Tis not fair for the bowl." She took the bowl, feeling his hand and trapping him in her stare. It had been a month. She'd watched him sleep on the floor night after night. Now, she now realized that what she'd felt stewing under the surface was his discouragement. She knew what it felt like to endure injustice, and she knew that soon he would succumb to the darkness as she had.

Again, she felt the flare; again, the fighting.

He tipped his head back, staring at the ceiling for several seconds, a familiar-to-Arianna-heaviness starting in his throat.

She wasn't sure why she wanted him to recognize what she had long known – that there was no hope and people were cruel even if they did pretend to be nice.

His sadness was poignant, more so than hers because it was strange to him. He'd not yet submitted to the dull understanding of hopelessness.

She closed her hand tighter over his, telling herself she should relish this moment.

But something stronger than the darkness shot through him again, and when he lowered his face, he was smiling. It was a stiff smile, but a smile nonetheless.

With gusto, he grabbed her hand, kissing the back of it like he was still a king.

"But now the bowl can meet the beautiful little mouse that lives in the kitchen –" He smiled, and the darkness was completely gone.

Arianna swallowed. Now, she was the one caught. "B -but what does a bowl have for a mouse?" she whispered.

"Well, he now has all the kitchen scraps so the mouse and bowl are doing well."

"You are impossible to dissuade!"

She stepped back, and he chuckled. "Then why do you keep trying?"

"I -"

Edgily, she tried to push her hair back into her bun, but he'd stepped closer to her, his gaze rising to her hair. "Why do you pull your hair so tight?"

"To keep it out of my face."

"It's still in your face." His voice had lowered.

She caught her breath as she watched him reach out, taking one loose strand around his finger, his expression softening as he stared at the loose tendril.

Slowly, she raised her hand to pull his finger down, but instead stood, her hand cupping his hand up by her ear, feeling his reverence – for her.

"I don't want – touch." She whispered, the lie obvious as she held tightly to his hand, awed and foggy.

"Really?" He smiled without breaking her trance. "Do you wish to know what I think? I think you want it very deeply. Mayhap, you want many things very deeply, but won't admit it."

"That isn't true." She knew she should let go to prove him wrong but couldn't bring herself to.

"I've proof." He smiled, the cocky expression back. "I know you like to touch. You touch me on purpose several times a day."

She hadn't realized how obvious she'd been, and it frustrated her.

She jerked her hand back, almost stumbling over the make-shift bed in the corner and then sat primly at the table and glared at him.

"What do you want?" He laughed, sitting in front of his pasty.

"What?"

"You claim you don't want a great many things. What do you actually want?"

"To survive today -"

"No, you are too passionate a person, Aria, to want just today. What do you dream of? What do you want?"

She stared at him, the man who made all the things she thought were safety feel like darkness and all her understanding of the world look like hate.

For years, all she'd wanted was his destruction.

She'd wanted his castle burned, his people homeless and his family gone – like hers.

But she wasn't sure she wanted it anymore, and now, what did she want?

She wanted to have the happiness and joy that lived in him and to know how he fought the darkness, but she knew such power could not be hers for the sacrifice would be too great.

"I don't know what I want," she finally whispered.

"Then I have a solution for you." He leaned forward, his eyes twinkling, but his tone growing serious.

"What is that?"

"Follow me."

Her heart flipped, and she almost wanted to, but instead she glared at him. "You are sitting."

"Aye. But follow me." His face broke into his best smile.

"I don't understand. Tell me what you mean," Arianna demanded instinctively reaching her hand out and grabbing his again.

"You don't know what you want," he started.

"I – well –"

"You said as much."

"True."

"And you are fickle, Aria. You claim you want no touch but touch me several times a day. You claim you wish to not share a bed, but I oft' find you watching me and -"

She felt frustration under the surface, but he pushed on. "And you claim to not like the villagers – but I know you always eavesdrop on my conversations with them."

She dropped her gaze. Did the man miss anything?

He continued. "So, follow me, and I'll show you what you want."

"You are very confident."

"I am."

She pulled back, and he sighed. "But why are you afraid to follow?"

"I'm not afraid of anything."

He scoffed. "You are afraid of everything. You are so afraid you won't even hope."

"I've just learned it is *foolish* to hope."

Marc's voice softened. "Nay. You are afraid, but you don't have to be afraid. I'll protect you."

He spoke with such absolute sincerity that he almost looked believable – as he had thirteen years before.

Slowly, she raised her chin, forcing her gaze past him to the hearth bricks. He'd broken his promise that night, and he'd not come back. He'd left her there in her burning castle to die.

"I don't need protection. I've survived well on my own."

He sighed and rose, walking back toward the yard. "You've survived Aria, but until you can hope, you'll never have the courage to do more than survive."

She stared after him. He was wrong. He wouldn't protect her. He had betrayed her once, and he'd do it again.

It was best that she'd betray him first.

CHAPTER 10

MONTH TWO

*D*o not strain your leg, Aria!" Marc snatched his wife up, amazed again at her lightness as he marched toward a bench he'd put in next to a few little blueberry bushes he'd dug up from the woods.

It had been two months since Aria's broken leg, and he knew he was overreacting. Her leg was likely healed, but he would not risk her straining herself as long as he was present.

He'd expected her to protest, but instead she tipped her head back, resting it on his arm and giggled. "But then you wouldn't carry me!"

She laughed again, closing her eyes, and Marc stopped mid-stride, staring down at her.

It was the first time he'd heard her truly laugh,

and it was so different than what he'd expected. It was deep and full – and completely from her heart.

"I knew I'd love your laugh, and I do," he said softly.

She opened her eyes and then stilled. Her normally hard face softened, and hesitantly, she raised one hand to his neck, the last rays of the evening's sun, making her glow in his arms.

This was the moment he'd been waiting for. He'd planned to kiss her for so long, and now she was ready. All he needed was to pull her to him. She'd come, and they'd finally be one.

But as he stared into her too-dark eyes, something in him recoiled, and he unexpectedly felt trapped which was foolish. He was in control. She was responding to him and his weeks and weeks of wooing.

But regardless, he couldn't kiss her. Not now.

With finality, he set her on the bench and stepped back.

"You are almost healed, but one misstep could set you back another few months." He sterned his voice, trying to ignore what had just happened, but as she turned her face away, he saw the damage he'd done.

He should have kissed her. They'd been married two months, and she had been waiting.

Why hadn't he just kissed her?

Frustrated, he knelt down to unwrap the bandage as if to prove that there could be swelling.

There wasn't, but he made a show of wrapping it back up.

"It's bad when it isn't quite healed and rebreaks. I saw it a few times in D'argent where they had to fight and old wounds weren't healed yet."

Her gaze snapped back. "You were in D'argent during the war?"

Relieved to have distracted her, Marc nodded. "Aye. I traveled with Petir in the worst part of it for five months."

Two months ago, Arianna would never have believed that there could be more to spoiled, selfish spendthrift Marc Simmins, but now it made so much sense about him.

"You were *allowed* to travel with Petir?"

"Yes and no. I traveled with him for five months, the summer I turned fifteen. I was staying with Uncle Amis at the palace. Well, the *remains* of the palace in D'argent. I was angry and spoiled –"

"I'm sure you were not."

"I was. I assure you. I hated my father and uncle for what they'd done, and I guess I hated myself a good deal too. I really just hated for the sake of hate. It starts to feel comfortable in the darkness of it after a while."

Arianna nodded. She knew that better than he could guess.

"Well, after a few days of dealing with me, Uncle Amis marched me down to the physician and the physician's apprentice -"

"Petir?"

"Aye, he was twenty-one then though he seemed so much older."

Marc paused, and she thought he'd stop, but he was staring off into the distance. "It was just after the winter battles with the fleet of pirates from the Jade Isles, and it was a cold spring. The pirates had left the city in ruins, and every day, the physician was traveling all over the city and the neighboring villages seeing what he could do to help the poor people. There were almost no supplies for him, but he did his best."

Arianna found it difficult to believe Marc's uncle would put his nephew, the crown prince, in such danger. It was so risky!

Marc shook his head slowly. "The needs were

endless, but Petir kept telling me to "plant hope." I felt like I poured into an abyss, but I learned to pour – and to reach out and feel their pain."

She fought to keep her face placid. She'd never guessed he'd cared enough to feel the pain of her people, and she wished it didn't soften her so much.

"They weren't even your people, Marc. Why did you —?" She paused fearing she'd give away too much.

"I had to. I had to know them. Aye, I hated it, but I stopped thinking so much of myself and started thinking of them, and it changed me — though it was hard."

"It was dangerous for your uncle to have sent you though – especially since you were heir to the throne."

"That's what father said. After a couple months, a few hungry scavengers tried to attack us. I'd not known Petir could fight, but he fought them off. We were all pretty bruised up. Father found out about my adventures and whisked me back to Terram, never allowing me back to D'argent though Thomis stayed with Uncle Amis two more years."

He stood, heading toward the chickens, Smiles racing after him, eager to grab his own seeds from the feed.

Arianna watched him, wishing she'd not asked him about his past.

CHAPTER 11

MONTH THREE

Three months had passed, and the autumn fair had come. The capital of Terram had quintupled in size and was unrecognizable.

Colorful banners waved above, and portable booths had popped up between every building while delicious smells of baked goods, cinnamon, and chocolate mixed together in the air.

Arianna was glad for the chaos. There were enough extra visitors that even she and Marc could walk down the main street and barely be noticed.

The people of Terram who did recognize them were open to wave to Marc, their beloved king turned one of them, and a few had even started to give her hesitant smiles.

She breathed out, surprised at how natural it felt to walk beside him, and she tipped her head up, letting herself do something she had been doing more and more – enjoy life.

It was like the things around her had started to take color, and the people looked prettier and less rough. Her leg had healed, and she was walking without a limp and more miraculously without pain.

They had come to the center of town and paused, and she realized Marc was staring at the town clock, the one that had sealed Marc's fate and reduced him to being a tanner.

Her stomach flipped.

She'd felt a growing turmoil in him when they touched, and despite all his flirting, he hadn't kissed her yet - not that she should want him to kiss her. She didn't, of course.

"It must bring back hard memories." She tried carefully, steeling herself for the answer.

He shrugged. "Aye. I was just thinking of a very hard memory. It just came to me though I hadn't thought of it in a long time."

Arianna's heart sank. "It was only three months ago."

"Nay." He sighed. "I was thinking of a memory from twelve years ago."

Marc gestured toward clock. "When I was 9, I snuck from the castle with Thomis, and we came down to the church. One of the kitchen maids had told us that if we rang the bell at exactly midnight, we could talk to one person who had died. We rang the bell, but all it did was bring out the night watchman. He grabbed us both by the scruffs of the necks and was about to throttle us for our mischief when he realized who we were! He was so stunned and apologetic, and he not only let us go but helped us get back into the castle the next day by distracting the guard at the gate for us."

He sent her one of his most boyish smiles, and wrapped his big, warm hand around one of hers.

The image of the poor night watchman trying to help the two disobedient princes was ridiculous. Arianna giggled as the warmth - and relief - spread over her.

"Thomis went with you?" she challenged. She could see Marc skirting the rules, but she'd never imagine Thomis doing it.

"He was different then. It was when Thomis stayed in Caedoline in D'argent with Uncle Amis that he changed."

She took a deep breath. "Did you try to speak to someone dead?"

His smile faded, and he forced a shrug. "I had a childhood friend who died. I thought – Well, I wanted to tell her something."

Arianna knew instantly he was speaking of her, and the warmth heated. How open was her face? She could barely breathe.

"Tell her what?"

How she wanted to know!

He was still smiling, but it was forced now, and there was a throbbing that was coming from somewhere as he stared past her. "It was a long time ago, but she was killed - in the war, the first night when the palace caught fire. I always wished I could have gone back to get her, but they grabbed me, and I always wished I could have told her I was sorry."

Sorry.

He'd said it. But more than that, he'd cared, and grieved, and tried to make it right in his own childish way.

"The funny thing is, I spent years looking for her - even though I knew she was dead, but I haven't the last few months. I feel settled when I'm with you Aria, in a way I never thought I could feel again. But seeing the tower just now, I just remembered how driven I was to find her for so long.

He was smiling, but the throbbing between them was rising.

"You loved her."

He shook his head. "We were eight years old, Aria. We liked getting into trouble and playing tricks on her simple-minded old nurse."

Arianna had forgotten about that, and she giggled again.

He dragged her toward him, planting a playful kiss on her forehead. "And if I'd married that girl, you'd not have gotten your handsome and kingly husband who is so terrible at tanning skins."

"You're not -" Arianna murmured, pulling back. "- so terrible."

"I am, but I have improved."

"Aye, that you have." She took another step back. "Who was your friend who was killed?"

Marc shrugged. "She was the princess of D'argent before – the war. Her name was Arianna."

"Arianna?" she asked, loving the sound of her full name on his lips and wishing he'd say it again.

"Aye." He was looking back at the tower "I've oft' thought of how her name is so similar to yours, and there have been moments -" He broke off before giving her a crooked grin. "But you are very different from her."

"How?" Arianna demanded.

"Well, your eyes."

She nodded. Casimir was the only one who knew

her eyes had changed color, slowly darkening over the last thirteen years. She didn't know why or how, but she'd been glad. The gold was transparent. She had not wanted to be transparent.

"Just my eyes?" She pushed, knowing she shouldn't. She should distract him and tell him that she was the furthest thing from a princess, but instead she pressed him.

He shifted. "She laughed a great deal."

"She was rich!"

But the excuse fell short for Marc laughed daily, and he was poor.

"Aria! Enough! She was a child who liked to tease and dance." He started to turn away, but suddenly, inexplicably, Arianna wanted to prove she was still the girl he'd been enchanted with.

Grabbing his arm, she marched toward the dancers, dragging him with her.

She'd never have done it if she didn't want to believe that the girl was still inside her somewhere, and when she reached the square, she paused at the side, watching the boisterous villagers and remembering why she hadn't danced in three years.

Dancing took feeling.

Feeling hurt.

Marc had stopped protesting and now sensed her hesitance.

"Don't be afraid, Aria."

"Do you forget I *was* a dancer?" she snapped.

"Have you danced since you fell?"

Her eyes warmed. "No."

Another thing she had held precious, taken in the space of a breath.

He slipped his hand into hers, sending the longed-for spurts of warmth that always accompanied his touch.

She held on, holding to the feelings a little longer, and he was smiling at her as he slid his arms around her waist, and somehow, they'd moved into the square, the soft grace easy on her feet.

"Dance with me." He murmured. She closed her eyes, hearing the melody.

It was an old, loved folk song, danced by a dozen generations before them and sewn into the fabric of Marc's people.

For the first time in years, Arianna felt the draw of the air – not to use – but to enjoy.

She thrust her hand out, bending the air and making it rivel in a sweeping circle around them.

She wanted to dance.

She pressed into his chest, trying to resist the pull of the air. But his heart beat in rhythm with his feet, and it drew her even more.

This was not just a dance; it was the hopes and

dreams of the people of Terram. Brides had danced this dance at their weddings. Children had zig-zagged through the dancers. Old men had clapped in rhythm to the time.

The rhythm was hardier than the rhythm of her own people. Her people's folk songs used more flutes and fifes, their lilting calls sounding as mystical as the wind with an undercurrent of rhythm, like the lapping of the sea.

Marc's music was steady and endless like his people's faithfulness. 1000 farmers, tilling their soil. 1000 mothers, spinning thin lines of wool and flax.

It was not refined and ethereal like D'argent. It was raw and natural like Terram.

Within this song, Marc's people were no longer enemies. They were families, communities and people with dreams - just like her people.

Their love and laughter coursed through her, and then she also felt their pain. Decades they worked, trying to build a future for their children and holding together their little towns by shear will in their little land-locked kingdom, a kingdom her father had enslaved with fees and taxes –

She stopped herself.

"No." she murmured.

"Feel with me." Marc breathed in her ear.

"I can't."

"You can. You are just resisting it. Follow me. *Follow.*"

He pulled her out from him, still holding her hands, and as he spun her, she felt the air calling – to give in to and leap higher and higher – and she was.

Oh, she'd forgotten the feel, this pulsing rhythm, combined with the whooshing of the air spinning around and within.

She was spinning, but she wasn't alone. The rest of the fair had disappeared, and she was spinning with Marc. It was like the night they'd flown together. He could read her every movement, and they were one in the dance.

This was so much better than when she danced alone before her leg had broken. She wasn't alone but with him, and they were navigating the dance, twirling through life, cutting through the air – together.

She knew she had to stop. Her leaps were too high, but all she wanted was to spin with him.

Forever.

She stopped so fast, he would have crashed into her if he could not read her so well.

And then they were standing alone with a circle of villagers around them.

Had everyone stopped to watch them?

She turned in terror to look at the smiling on-lookers.

Had her feet stayed on the ground?

The villagers began to clap and cheer, and re-gaining herself, Arianna took a step back from Marc, gently pulling her hand out of his. The pressure released, but she needed to escape. "I – I must – see - someone about - a skin."

And then she turned and ducked into the crowd

She needed a moment alone. The longer she was with Marc, the more confused she became.

She was at the edge of the town now, standing be-side the far stable, breathing in deeply despite the smell of manure when something gripped her arm, and she was dragged around the corner into the far side of the stable wall just out of view of the crowd.

"What are you doing?" Casimir's breath was hot, and his eyes blazed.

Fool! Searched for and wanted with a bounty on his head, and here he stood, angry as a bull.

"You should not be here!" she hissed.

"Of course, I should be here! The autumn ball is a week away, and we've found a way into the castle."

They'd found a way in? Arianna's throat tightened.

Casimir's mouth moved to a straight line. "But 'twould seem you are too busy dancing with our enemy to remember our goals."

"He's my husband!"

"You married him -"

"I had no choice!"

"You did!" He'd always had strange grey eyes that grew stormy when he was angry, but now they were turned on her, and Arianna found herself looking into hurricanes.

His voice stabbed. "The day the soldiers came, you knocked over the caldron which stopped me from saving you. You *chose* him."

"I – it was for the rebel cause – to get into the castle."

His face contorted. "My men have watched you. You have feelings for the killer of our people."

"Marc is no killer."

Casimir's hand tightened around her arm. "Do you not care about the glory of our people? Do you not remember that the kings of Terram toppled the house of Thrush? Remember your people. Remember when we were in our glory - "

Somewhere deep within her, the queen grasped her crown.

"Fie on glory when the children beg in the streets."

Casimir swallowed. He knew. He knew what war would do – and who would truly pay.

Her words came faster, and she was straightening. "Do I want the glory due our people? Aye! Of course, but not as much as I want peace. I want the children to have the homes that we never had. That is what I want!"

She stared into him, recognizing some of the same deep sorrow that daily plagued her. "Would you sacrifice the innocent for glory, Casimir?"

He was silent for several seconds, but when he spoke, his words were laced with passion. "You are a fool if you think the people of Terram will not stop rubbing our faces in the dung."

She started to shake her head, but he grabbed her chin, making her look at him.

"The treaty is a trick. I've spent the last couple months on the coast. I slipped onto the Ecoptian ambassador's ship. I heard their plan. They are going to use the treaty to enslave all the people under the Simmins' rule."

She stilled. "They wouldn't. Marc wouldn't."

"Maybe he would not, but what of his brother?

His uncle? They pander to the enemies of D'argent. They will sacrifice our people for their own safety."

She searched his face. He thought he spoke truth, but he must have misunderstood.

"You don't speak the language of the Jade Isles. You can't have heard correctly, and you are terrible with languages." But even as she said it, something nibbled at her memory. Hadn't Casimir always done better with the coastal languages? It was here, in Terram, the kingdom of the earth that he struggled. He was in his soul a man of the sea, even understanding their very language better. She had seen it time and time again when they were in the coastal cities, a part of him that she didn't understand came alive there —

"Aria."

Marc's voice.

Her chin was still encased in Casimir's grip, and she could only move her eyes to see Marc standing to her right.

Casimir saw him too, but waited a few seconds before moving.

Slowly, a pleased smirk lifting Casimir's lips, he let her go and stalked past Marc, jabbing Marc with his shoulder as he passed.

She stood, cold with fury – and something else.

Guilt. No. She had nothing to feel guilty about.

"What were you doing?" Marc demanded, his face

had gone white though she could not tell if it was shock or rage.

"I – I – oh, why should you care?"

"You're my wife!"

But she wasn't. He'd held back, not even kissing her. They weren't truly husband and wife.

She stood as tall as she could, glaring up at Marc.

"You know that's a lie!"

"It's not, Aria." He spoke with conviction. "You are my wife."

There were no words. She simply had to be away and reason left her.

She ducked around the corner of the stable out of his view and flew with all her might into the forest.

Marc rounded the corner and reached his hand out to grasp her, but his fingers caught air, and then he was standing alone behind the stable.

She could not possibly have run so fast. She'd been there a mere second before –

He stood, turning slowly. The tree line was several seconds away – even for him running at his fastest, and the roof was two stories above.

But where? He couldn't even think where she'd go.

She was gone, and like the whole past hour, nothing made sense.

The dance, the man -

Marc's mind scrambled over all he was realizing.

The dance had been strange.

He was a good dancer, but in himself, he could not have danced that well.

Yet, when he'd lifted, her, she'd been so light. When they'd spun together, the air had whirled with them.

It was like we were flying.

But more than that, they'd been unified, each reading each other without needing to think. The only time he'd ever experienced anything like it was the night he'd flown with Princess Arianna.

Was it possible that the One Father had given him another soul mate?

Even as his heart rejoiced at the thought, it sank again.

He'd just found his wife behind a building with a known rebel, and it had not surprised Marc as much as he wished it had.

Aria hid something from him behind her veiled gaze and placid face.

Not only did she know the rebels, the way the

rebel Casimir had looked at her angered Marc to his core.

She was intimately close to that dangerous man, and Marc was finished with her evasiveness.

Aria would give him answers. Marc would take no less than the full truth.

CHAPTER 12

*M*arc crossed the yard to the cottage with a heavy heart.

He'd have to wait for Aria to return home, but he had walked the length of the fair and had not found his wife.

Smiles waited in his favorite, sunny spot, rising immediately as he always did when Marc came back looking for a new plant or leaf Marc would pick on the way home for him.

"Sorry, Smiles." Marc sighed.

The gelada paced around him, expectantly, and Marc picked a long blade of grass, handing it to Smiles who happily trotted off with it.

Not a smart creature, but loyal and true – and likely the only company he'd have tonight. Somehow, he didn't feel Aria wished to speak to him and would take a long time to arrive home.

He was wrong. As he pushed the door open, he stood stunned.

She was sitting on the bed, her expressionless face staring at that empty place to the right of the hearth.

How?

There was no physical way she could have made it before him. Had someone brought her on a horse? Had Casimir -?

But he realized he didn't care, he slammed the door, and it made the small cottage shake as it banged shut.

He saw her grimace, but she didn't look up.

Arianna had hoped he'd take longer. She wasn't ready for the questions he was going to demand.

Instinctively, she crossed her arms, glaring at him, trying to show him she felt no guilt, but his first question wasn't what she expected.

"How is your leg?" He strode forward, reaching down to feel it. "'Twas foolish to run home, Aria. It's only just healed."

It wasn't as bad as he thought. She'd flown.

Nervous at feeling him, she jumped up.

"Sit!" he snapped.

She sat instantly, angry at herself for complying. Wretch, proud, demanding...

He'd dropped to his knee in front of her, feeling her shin. "It feels a little swollen. I'm concerned this will set you back."

"Why should you care?" She blinked furiously, unsure if she was asking about his stubborn insistance on caring at all or asking about her leg, but her question goaded him.

"Your choices affect both of us!" He glowered.

"So?" She hissed defensively.

Marc spread his free hand in frustration, and across the room, a pot flew from the tripod, crashing to hearth.

Arianna froze. She'd long feared he'd accidentally use the air powers when they touched, and he just had.

But by a miracle, Marc missed it. He was staring at her leg, his face pinched.

Slowly, he looked up at her, his voice controlled but the emotion stirring just beneath the surface. "How do you know the man, Casimir?"

She swallowed. "He is a friend to those in need."

"He manipulates the needy to his side. I have had

spies watching him for years. He is dangerous and wicked, Aria. You need to stay away from him."

Aria went cold.

Where had Marc been when she'd been vulnerable and in need of protection?

Where was he when his father had killed her family?

It had been Casimir who had been there as she'd sailed away from her home, friendless -save him, and ten years later, he'd been the one to leave the gypsies and stay with her in Terram when she'd broken her leg.

"He was there for me and others many times. Certes, you were not!"

"I am here now, and you do nothing but shut me out!" He stood.

"I do not want to be in debt to you!" she snapped, teetering on her perch on the bed and waving her finger towards his chest.

He grabbed her hand, and despite his anger, she felt his sorrow as he stood there holding her hand up to his chest. "I never considered you to be. I did it all out of –"

Love.

She knew it. Even in her rage, she paused, willing him to admit what she already knew.

Instead, she felt him dive back into his anger. "Do

you think I like cooking? I never asked anything back, but you never gave so much as a thank you - never a single thanks in three months."

With his free hand, he motioned around the room, and once again, a gust of wind hit the edge of the room, knocking several items over.

This time he noticed, and he turned, staring at the corner.

No, he couldn't discover it now. Not now, not when he'd only know the bad parts.

Arianna could barely breathe.

She had seconds before he'd realize, and then he'd remember about the soul connection, realize he'd had no choice but to marry her, and certes, he'd guess what she'd done to plot against him and his family with the rebels.

And then...he'd –

He'll leave.

He'd abandon her again. And in her heart, she was that child again on the side of the burning garden, alone, sent out into the dark, cold night.

Despite all her precautions, Marc had done it again. He taken her heart, and he was going to break it.

But this time, she had weapons. He had handed her his secrets. She knew his deepest regrets, and she would wield those against him. She had to!

She rose to her tallest height. "Marc Simmins, you are owed no thanks! You know what your family did to the coast. Would you take everything and give back a bit?"

"A bit?" He scoffed in a tone she'd not guessed him capable. "I was building back all that was taken, Aria. I devoted my reign to it. My kingdom was doing well!"

"Because you Simmins attacked and looted the kingdom of your allies!"

"Allies? We were practically their slaves, given how high their tolls were. One half of our goods to bring to sea, and one half the profit coming back. We'd make a quarter of our profit if we did well. Our people could barely put bread on their tables!"

"And so, your father brought down their king, killed their nobles -"

"What care you, Aria? You are one of us. You profit from their fall!"

She could barely breathe. It was the way with the Simmins, always assuming the worst of others! Never realizing their own sins. Wretch! Self-righteous fool!

The heat from her hate pulsed through her, demolishing her care, and she stumbled toward him. "Then it shows you don't know me at all. I am no traitor. You Simmins are the murderers!"

It felt like he got taller as his anger grew. "Do you say I am?"

The added fury filled her, and she stoked it gladly, his roughness strengthening her.

"The blood of your father runs in your veins. 'Twas he who pretended friendship — only to take down the house of Thrush by trickery and deceit!"

His face was white. "Thrush struck first; not Simmins."

She knew the lie, but she'd been there. The Simmins had struck first.

Her body was going numb, and she almost shook. "So you say, but I've seen the coast. You Simmins started a war that destroyed the lives of thousands!"

"Would you ask me to pay for the sins of my father?"

"Aye – I would." She could not think how he could do it, but she wanted it from him. She'd wanted it for years, and now she stared up at his face which was red with rage and told him.

He stood several seconds staring back before slowly spreading his hands in defeat. "I can't fix it, Aria. I tried. You can't imagine how much I tried when I was king, and now, I have no power to fix it."

He laughed, and his misery was so heavy in the air that it hurt.

She should be glad, but she wasn't.

Instead, she stood, waiting for him to leave.

But he didn't leave. He stood like a big tree, unmovable before her.

She could practically imagine the slice marks she'd purposely put in his trunk, but he wouldn't move. He was rooted into something inexplicably strong.

When he spoke next, his voice was completely firm. "I will not fight you, Aria."

She closed her eyes. She needed to strengthen the wall, but she could not. She'd spent all her strength, and he refused to pour more hate in.

Instead, Marc pulled her to himself, wrapping her in a gentle hug, and she knew her fight was over.

Deep inside herself, she heard the crack.

The wall had cracked.

She felt him jerk.

He could feel it.

There was a throbbing.

Marc held tighter to his wife.

A miracle was happening. For the first time, he could feel her feelings.

The throbbing came again, and it was getting stronger like a pumping behind a dam.

Finally. Finally!

He jerked her closer. Her feelings were there – just beyond his grasp.

He'd not let her go

She tipped her head back, her eyes wide, but she didn't pull back.

He reached deeper. They were there – so close -

And then something in her cracked.

It was small. He could feel so little…

But it was sharp…and horrible.

Like a jolt of lightening, Marc was hit hard enough that he started to stagger back, but he held fast to her.

It was she who jerked away. "Don't – don't touch me." she seethed. "I – I don't want you to!" She swung around pacing away from him and then turned again, staring at him with angry, accusing eyes.

Why? Why the anger and why her shame? He didn't understand. He backed away slowly ducking through the cottage door and into the darkening evening.

Leaving her.

Alone in the cottage, Arianna stood trembling.

She needed his love; she starved for it and needed it to thaw the ice that trapped her.

But for the first time, she realized she didn't deserve it.

But she needed it. It hurt too bad without it. She stood, staring after him,

It had never occurred to her to fear that he would feel the hate that was in her. The protection spell had always held, but it had cracked.

Frantically, she tried to dash the feelings back, but she knew it was too late.

Marc had felt what she was...

A monster.

No. Not her! It was the Simmins!

But the excuse that had always sustained her fell short.

She was the one who had spent over a decade planning vengeance.

She was the one who had married a man, knowing he had no choice.

She was the one who had dived over and over into her hate to justify her plans to destroy him and Terram.

Terram.

How long had she practiced hating these people who her father had starved with his levies?

And now Marc knew some of it, just a little, and he'd been rightly repulsed.

"Then let him be," she whispered bitterly.

Maybe she'd destroyed the marriage, but what marriage had it been? It had never had a chance; they were too different. She was a child of the air, and did not "Terram" mean land? He was a child of the land.

Once every thousand years, two souls are entwined, uniting the powers of the kingdoms.

The prophecy taunted her. Wasn't it obvious the Great Father had made a mistake?

Could He make mistakes?

She'd stopped shaking enough to sit in the lonely chair, watching the door.

Would he dare come back now that he'd sensed what was in her? Did she want him to?

She lowered her forehead to the table, aware that several tears, the first she'd shed in thirteen years puddled on the rough wooden top.

Marc walked into the woods, not caring where he was going.

He had given and given, first to his ungrateful

people who would not give him the mercy of a minute.

Then he had given and given to his wife.

"Who hates me," he admitted.

He knew what he had felt inside her.

Hate, numbing ice, and hate was like love: it permeated every other feeling. He hadn't felt much, but he knew enough to guess. She was filled with it, defined by it.

This was the truth of why he'd held back. It was why he'd not kissed her – protecting himself.

Though he'd not been able to feel her emotions until now, in his soul, he'd known she hated him.

Hadn't he seen that same expression of veiled loathing in the eyes of almost every D'argentian he'd met during the war?

Aye. He had.

And now that he knew, it made sense that she was close to someone like Casimir, a rebel and a D'argentian.

Because Aria is a D'argentian too.

He knew it as sure as he breathed. It showed in her knowledge of the coast and the soft accent that cradled her words when she wasn't thinking. Of course, she was a D'argentian, and how much more?

How much had she done with the rebels?

And now, this woman who hated him was demanding that he pay for sins that were not his?

To sacrifice himself?

He *had* sacrificed — again and again — but now, to sacrifice for a wife who would never love him back?

What did he even have left to give?

They'd taken his crown and his kingdom.

What was left?

His heart?

No. Somehow Aria already had his heart. She'd had it before he remembered giving it.

What was even left to give?

Marc walked farther into the forest. There was something he was holding onto with the last remnants of his strength, and it was what he'd been afraid to give up.

My pride.

His pride was all that was left.

To go in now and offer love when he knew all he'd get back was hate was insane.

He'd be a fool to give now.

Marc came to the edge of the woods, realizing with surprise that he'd walked in a circle and was back at the clearing that opened to the meadow beside the tannery.

The evening sky was striped with pink and orange, tinted with deep purples.

Marc studied the beauty of it, too deep in sorrow to form words to pray but finding his soul weeping before the One Father.

The One Father raised the sun over those who loved Him and those who hated Him.

But more than that, the Son of the One Father had sacrificed Himself — even though he'd been hated — and in the power of the One Father's love for Marc, not Marc's love for the One Father, Marc had been set free.

Love freed.

And it had been an unearned gift, and now, Marc was called to extend it to his hurting wife.

On the day of their marriage, he promised to love her, and his promise had not been only to her, but to a higher Power.

Now, standing in the same place that he had resolved to accept his life as a tanner, he had to return to the same vow from his marriage ceremony – even if she didn't love him back.

If he looked like a fool, so be it. His hope was not in her, but in the One he'd made the promise to.

The last of his pride slipped away, and in its place came a sweet, refreshing peace that filled him completely making his fears look petty compared to the power of the One Who loved him and called Him to love.

And the calling to love his broken, hurting wife no longer seemed hard but natural and obvious.

He stood worshiping several minutes before he turned back to the cottage with a sure step.

He would sacrifice more - against all reason and for a woman who hated him.

With resolve, he pulled the cottage door open.

Aria stood in the center of the room, and she raised her chin defiantly as she glared at him, but this time, Marc saw past himself and his pain enough to see hers.

Give.

He crossed to her slowly, not taking his eyes from her face.

"I love you, Aria," he whispered.

And he did - not just as a husband, but as a soul seeing her soul, aching, and in need of a love he could give, and he would.

He would give.

Arianna was sure Marc was insane.

Trembling, she felt his hand.

The love was not just a feeling; it was a determination. It was impossible, absurd, but she couldn't deny it because it was filling every pore of her. It was no longer only the warmth but a peace – and a *hope, a life-giving hope.*

She'd never dreamed this kind of feeling existed. It was more wonderful than anything she'd thought possible, and she knew she didn't deserve this peace, not with all the hate she still held on to.

"You shouldn't," she murmured, grabbing his hand with both of hers.

"I should."

Hadn't he felt the crack?

"I love you," he said firmly. And she knew he meant it, and he was going to kiss her – and more.

He shouldn't, but she needed him to.

She needed love, even while knowing she didn't deserve it.

Didn't one love something because of its worth? She had none. Everything she'd done in her life had been meant to destroy this man who willingly offered the thing she so desperately needed.

He brought love. She brought hate.

But her need was too great. She closed her eyes and gave into the warmth.

CHAPTER 13

FRIDAY

One week of happiness. One week of tasting love.

It was richer and deeper than she would have imagined.

It would not last, and yet, to think that it had been hers for a week, one precious, beautiful week of love and happiness.

Of course, even when he touched her, the happiness wasn't complete.

Even as his joy filled every corner of her, an emptiness fought back like a shadowy, murky darkness within the light.

But for one, beautiful week, love had been hers, and it had been so full, she thought it might be enough to last her an entire lifetime.

And now it's over, she admitted to herself, for tonight was the autumn ball.

She turned to see Marc step through the door, the afternoon sun, making his hair glow orange. Without a second thought, Arianna rose to kiss him, slipping her hands into his and sighing into the warmth.

He kissed her gently and then looked around, a tremor of pleasure spurting through him that made her smile when she felt it.

"It looks different in here."

She shrugged, admiring her own work. She knew the cottage had transformed. Soft light blue curtains blew at the windows, and a few flowers were tied with ribbon along the front of the mantle.

In the center of the table was a pot of the last of the wildflowers, and the table had a crisp white table cloth on it.

She glanced up and let herself bask in his delighted expression. "These things were left in the chest from the old owners. I just never bothered with a tablecloth before. It was more to clean." She paused, unsure why she'd needed to pull everything out now. She just had wanted to share the little bits of beauty with him though she could think of no rational reason why. "But now, I just wanted to make the cottage pretty."

He lowered his forehead down to hers. "The seeds are blooming."

She giggled "Quite the opposite. It's fall, Marc. They are dying."

"Not those seeds."

And from the way Marc looked at her, she hoped he was right.

His voice was casual, but his blood sped. "I have an errand to run."

Arianna was too relieved to wonder why he'd tensed. She had a much more serious errand. Now she'd be able to slip away to the rebel camp without Marc knowing.

If she could just talk to Casimir, she could dissuade him. Thankfully, she and Marc would be here, far from the battle, but she could not stop thinking of Brion, and the fat old cook, and the other castlefolk. She had to dissuade Casimir from attacking!

She looked back at Marc and found he was studying her. "I'd like to take you to the ball, tonight," he said.

She froze. *No.*

"But you are no longer king," she whispered, stunned that he intended to go.

"Half the town is going. Tanners can go."

"But, won't you be ashamed?"

She felt the tell-tale flare in his pulse when his

pride invaded the calm, but he gave her his cockeyed smile.

"I'd like to take you to an extravagant ball that I planned but don't have to pay for."

"We shouldn't go, Marc. We should stay away."

"Why?" His tone hardened instantly. "Is there danger?"

Arianna was caught. Surely, he didn't suspect she'd know anything about what the rebels meant to do – not with the gentleness and love he'd treated her with this week.

She looked down at her stiff brown skirt and found a lie he'd believe. "I just don't have anything to wear."

"Oh." His face fell. "Oh, of course. I had not thought of that. What a fool I am. Once I'd planned to buy you dresses in every color, and now, I cannot even buy you one."

She nodded emphatically. "It's alright. I want to stay here with you anyway."

She squeezed his hand, but she felt his heart was racing.

Did he not believe her, or was he upset that he could not buy her a dress?

"Mayhap, I can work something out," he breathed. "I'll be back in a couple hours."

Kissing her gently, he headed out the door. Arianna watched him stride into the woods, her heart pounding, almost as concerned about his mysterious errand as her own.

She only waited a minute before flying into the woods toward Casimir's camp.

Casimir had said he'd found a way in, but maybe she could go and dissuade him from his plans.

She had to at least try.

The camp had grown significantly, and tents and fire pits dotted the wooded hill in straight lines while a bustle of at least four dozen youths raced around the camp, preparing for whatever plans Casimir had laid out.

Arianna guessed Casimir had found young D'argentians to travel back with him. Only he could use a three-month exile to grow his following.

But what did he have planned? She circled before landing, scanning the camp. While most of the youths in the camp were D'argentian. Casimir always had a way of bringing young youths to his cause. A red-headed Terramite boy caught her eye for she remembered him from the town. Who was he? The miller's son? No. Which family had bright red hair? She tried to remember.

One thing at the center of the camp was the focus of the youths' attention. It was a brightly colored cart, and something very, very tall was in the cart — though she couldn't see what.

She landed, but as she walked toward the cart, Casimir came to greet her.

"You came." He smiled, but then stopped, searching her face, his gaze hardening. "Yet, you will not aid us."

She didn't move. "We shouldn't attack."

"The empty-headed Simmins are about to sign away their people. Now, we need to protect *our* people."

"It's not all the Simmins. It's Thomis; he took the throne from Marc."

Casimir's eyes flashed. "It was Marc; the contract was written months ago – in dragon's blood."

Dragon's blood.

Was Marc such a fool? In his pride – had he agreed to such a thing?

Casimir was staring hard into her. "It's a trap. There is something about the contract. The Ecoptians kept saying it is alive. They mean to enslave the kingdoms of the Simmins."

Arianna's mind raced. "If that's true, it will doom

both kingdoms, Terram and D'argent. The Simmins rule over both."

He took her hand. "Not the D'argent kingdom if you take your place as the queen of your people."

She stilled, and he pushed on. "You are the rightful heir. If you take your throne, D'argent will be saved."

She faltered. "I – I can't do that."

"It's exactly what you must do to save your people!" He burst before pausing, his voice lowering reverently. "*Queen Arianna.* Take your throne. Lead your people.

She paused several seconds, trying to think. What if the prophecy was real?

Could their mistakes ruin a destiny set before them a thousand years before they were born?

She looked up at Casimir. "What if our marriage was the fulfillment of the prophecy?"

Casimir paused, several emotions played across his face before he gentled, looking at her once again as her long-time friend. "You are closing your eyes to the darkness because you don't want to betray him. The prophecy is a blind hope."

Three months living with Marc had thawed Arianna enough to believe, and her words surprised her.

"Hope has eyes to see beyond the darkness."

He shook his head. "The prophecy is just a wives' tale. It isn't real."

Arianna rushed on. "But if Marc and I are connected, wouldn't that mean we are the fulfillment of the prophecy? When we touch, I – feel things I'd never known could be felt."

He pressed his lips together. "You sound like one of the girls of Terram who fawn over him –"

"We share powers."

His face paled. "You don't."

But she saw in his eyes, he almost believed her.

She nodded. "We do."

He took her shoulders, looking at her seriously. "Arianna, you must think of your people. Even if this prophecy is true, it's still too late to save his kingdom. He lost the crown, and now his foolish brother means to sign away the kingdom. Save your people. Put them first."

"And abandon the people of Terram and betray my husband?"

He stiffened. "You betray your people by loving our enemies!"

"I hope in love." She whispered stoutly, unsure how she dared.

"There is no hope in that for when the contract is signed both sides will fight for themselves."

"Then we need to stop the signing!"

"We?" he echoed with a harsh laugh.

"Yes." She stood as tall as she could. "As your queen I command you fight for peace, Casimir. Try to stop the signing"

She motioned past him to the youths, all between fourteen and twenty-five, the oldest surpassing Casimir in age but all looking to him for leadership to fix the broken world they'd inherited.

"You don't want them to have the life we had."

She saw him struggle for several seconds, but then he stepped back from her.

"I am teaching them not to be defeated by it." he growled. "I am leading them to regain the kingdom you lost while you openly love our enemy under the weak excuse of an old prophecy."

She faltered, and he stepped back. "And I see that I placed my hope in the wrong place when I hoped in you."

She saw the pain in his eyes, and she knew it was deeper than her rejection of the rebel cause.

But she could not comfort him in that.

Painfully, she turned and flew away.

Thomis sat behind the wide mahogany desk in the solar, the upper family room, and raised a single gold brow when Marc marched into the kingly solar, his clothing stinking of the tannery.

"Good morning, brother." Thomis paused to pen a column of numbers down the ledger.

"I have two things to speak to you about," Marc snapped.

"And I wish to speak to you." Thomis jabbed his finger into the page. "What did you order from the baker? He charged a hefty sum for this autumn ball cake. 'Twould appear from the price the cake is frosted with gold!"

"It's just large." Marc shrugged back his frustration. "But I suppose since you won't have the Jade Isles delegates -"

"They are still coming." Thomis' nostrils flared slightly.

"You still plan to sign the contract?" Marc was stunned. He thought he'd be relieved, but he wasn't. Somehow, Thomis choosing to sign with their kingdom as leverage felt more dangerous than when Marc himself was doing it.

Thomis was scowling. "Uncle Amis felt it would be wise to continue with the negotiations."

Marc digested this. He'd never liked Uncle Amis

since the night Arianna had been killed, and it added to his trepidation.

"You spoke to Uncle Amis when you were in D'argent?" Marc asked.

Thomis glared out the window. "Yes. Unlike you, brother, I seek council when I rule two kingdoms, and I spoke to him on my trip."

Marc ignored the jab. Looking back, he could see he'd been a bit arrogant, but there was nothing he could do now. He also wasn't sure Uncle Amis was a good counselor.

"He knows D'argent well." He would admit that much though no more. "He's lived there thirteen years now, and I can't imagine him ever leaving it."

"And yet, you shall have to, for he is here in Terram for the signing tonight."

Marc straightened. That was odd.

Thomis turned. "Now, you said you had two things to speak to me of. What were they?"

"I wanted one of mother's old dresses for Aria. She doesn't have a dress for the ball."

Thomis tipped his head to the side toward a chest in the corner, and Marc crossed to it, flinging it open.

None of the dresses were the right color for Aria. His mother had been fair and tall like himself, and she'd loved flowers and laughter. The dresses were heavily embroidered and all too long. Hesitantly, he pulled a bright blue one out and folded it up. It was the closest to Aria's taste, and it was still completely wrong.

"But," Thomis said slowly from behind. "I would prefer you not come tonight, brother."

Marc bunched the dress under his arm and crossed to the desk. "Everyone is invited!"

Thomis avoided his gaze. "Aye, I just think it may make us look weak. It will appear strange to our guests that the former king is now a tanner."

"Because it is strange. It is an unjust law!"

Thomis straightened. "I have a ball to prepare for, but you said you had a second thing you wished to speak of?"

Marc spoke through gritted teeth. "I wanted to tell you that I saw Casimir, the escaped rebel, at the fair."

"We've no doubt they will attempt something. Rest assured; we are more than ready."

"They will walk into a trap?"

"If they choose to try to take the castle, we will protect it – with more than they can imagine. Their leader, Casimir, is a flyer of the power of the Thrush. I will have a hundred men hiding on the wall ready to shoot him with arrows."

"But it should be a night of peace."

Thomis' nostrils flared. "Do you not understand

brother? No, of course not. That is why you married a tanner when we needed money and allies. You weren't supposed to marry her. You were supposed to marry Lillian."

"The governor's daughter?"

"You liked her."

"When I spoke to you, I always liked her, but then when I was not with you, I liked Aria."

His brother's face turned down. "That's not how it usually works."

"How what works?" Marc demanded.

Thomis stood, impatiently grabbing Marc's arm. "Forget we talked. Just go home, and realize how unimportant this is."

Marc felt calm immediately, and he nodded. This was unimportant.

But the fear that Aria was involved with the rebels pierced through. He couldn't forget and rest. The idea was ludicrous. He needed to pursue this; it was his duty to Aria to protect her!

He pulled his grip out of this brother's and instantly the calm left him.

Thomis' mouth was ajar. "Wait." He grabbed Marc's arm again.

The calm returned.

"Just forget it all." Thomis pressed his fingers deep into Marc's skin.

But now Marc knew.

Pushing through the haze of complacency, he managed to twist his arm free.

Again, the calm vanished.

He stared at Thomis.

"You lied," he whispered. "You *do* have powers."

His mind raced, trying to piece several years of clues together.

"You can control people through touch!" Marc gasped.

His brother reached for him again, his face pale.

Marc jumped back. "You even tried to make me marry someone I didn't love!"

Thomis shook his head. "You love the tanner?"

"Yes!" Marc shouted. "Your powers couldn't force me to deny who I loved. But would you steal that from me too, brother? Wasn't it you who stole my crown? You were there that night. You caused the priest to slow, didn't you?"

Thomis was so pale his lips had almost disappeared. "I didn't know you loved her. I – I thought you'd be happy as the governor's son. I didn't mean for you to be reduced to a tanner." He shook his head. "It was so perfectly planned, Marc, I only wanted the best for the kingdom. You know you were spending our resources. I just never could have guessed that her enchantment over you would cause you to resist my powers. Nothing else caused you to."

"Enchantment?" Marc growled. "Tis no enchantment to love someone."

"'Twas like you were bewitched, as if you were destined by some deep charm to marry a woman of such mean birth. Still, I thought you –"

"Destined?" Marc echoed.

"It was a power above anything I'd realized." Thomis looked miserable. "Forgive me, brother, but in my desire to protect the kingdom, I did not stop you. I fear she is a witch. Your actions were not rational when it came to her. There was this deeper magic that overpowered everything else."

Marc backed out of the room, not taking his gaze from his brother's miserable face.

Then he turned and ran.

Destined.

Could it be true?

He was running now and didn't stop until he reached the cottage. It was empty, and Marc looked around for any proof, his gaze finally falling on the hearth.

She always stared at these bricks – somewhere in the middle.

He raced to the hearth, searching the stones along its right side.

He pushed his fingers along their rough edges, but they felt tight.

Something, a clue. He needed it though he didn't know what he looked for –

And then one of the bricks gave ever so slightly.

Jerking out his sword, he pushed the blade between the bricks, not caring if he snapped the tip of the sword off.

The brick moved a bit more, and finally it wiggled enough that he could get it out.

There, at the back, was a small silk handkerchief of the finest fabric wrapped around a tiny object.

With trembling hands, he unwrapped the object and there, glinting in the semi-dark cottage was the ruby pin he'd given to Princess Arianna.

He laughed.

Arianna. My Arianna. Of course, it is you.

He studied the small ruby pin in his hand, tears of joy and anger warming his eyes.

She was alive – but was she?

The laughing, dancing princess was long gone, and in her place was a woman who could not hope.

What was more, she'd used their soul connection against him and lied to him repeatedly, likely working with the rebels to bring down his family.

Arianna soared to the door of the cottage, her mind still whirling.

Her feet had barely scraped the dirt when she jerked the door open and stopped short.

Marc sat in the semi-dark, his arm resting on the wooden table beside a small object that glinted with the single stream of light from the door.

He reached for her, and she came instantly, trying to read his expression, but as his hand closed over hers, she recognized the tiny object.

The ruby pin.

With his free hand he pushed his palm past her, creating a gust of wind that blew the door open the rest of the way, using the power as naturally as if he'd been born with it.

He knew.

The dreaded moment had come, and all Arianna wanted to do was escape it.

All terror channeled into the gust she aimed for his chest, but his grip only tightened.

"Arianna!"

He managed her real name through the torrent of air.

"Let go!" She cried.

But she felt his resolve, a cold calm pumping with anger.

So much anger. Had he also thought of the soul connection and realized that he'd had no choice but to marry her? Of course, he had.

Panicking, she shot upward, dragging Marc with her.

The cabin blurred in their speed, the air rushing around them in a whoosh that was ended by a loud crack.

It was his head.

She almost shrieked with a new fear, as they floated eighteen feet above the stone floor.

Had she hurt him? Would he fall?

But then he was clutching at a beam, shaking his head and grimacing, and the self-protection she'd so long fed, drove her back, twisting out of his grip in his moment of weakness.

She pushed several feet from him, floating in midair to make sure he was not so wounded that he'd fall.

"Aria – Arianna." He grasped the beam and reached for her.

"I – I'm sorry." She sputtered, backing toward the door.

"No!" He hollered, clambering down the beam toward the wall. She saw his gaze drop to the floor, measuring the distance. He meant to jump!

"Don't!" She screamed.

He leapt toward her straight into the air. Frantically she pushed the air up, thrusting it into him and thrusting him into the wall before he crashed to the floor.

He staggered up, but she was to the door now, and in seconds she was in the yard and had flown up to roof-height.

Marc raced out the door, his expression desperate. "Come down! We will talk."

She shook her head numbly. The happiness was over, but she had to warn him about the ambassador's treachery.

"The contract is a trap. You have to stop it from being signed."

He darkened instantly. "Did Casimir tell you that?"

The expression on his face wounded her to her core. She wished she could explain, but there was too much evil that was true. He'd never forgive her.

"I did — love you." She tried weakly.

His voice was deadly calm. "You couldn't love me. You loved hating me too much."

Tears filled her eyes, and she shot into the woods without looking back.

CHAPTER 14

*M*arc slumped next to the door holding his aching temples.

Smiles came over to check him, nuzzling Marc's bent head.

"My hair is not grass, Smiles." Marc sighed before staring up where his wife had disappeared.

All this time, he'd tried to plant seeds with his enemy, and what good had it done? Nothing that he could see. He wasn't sure the seeds had even been planted. It seemed they'd blown away in the wind.

Rising slowly, he turned into the cabin. He still had one duty left. He needed to go tonight and stop – whatever was about to happen.

Now, he realized the more imminent threat, one

he hated to admit. The rebels had their queen, and they'd have every reason to strike tonight.

Every D'argentian lord was in Terram; he'd invited them to the autumn ball. If the rebels attacked, Marc had brought the rebels' allies right into the heart of his castle, endangering his people. He had to warn Thomis.

Sensing his master's sadness, Smiles followed him into the cottage.

Marc changed into the clothes he'd worn the night he'd been married and tried to comb his unruly hair before heading toward the magical door, Smiles still close at his heals.

Half an hour later, he stepped through the glowing tunnel into the garden, the soft scents and distant lilting music a sharp contrast to the severity of his mission.

"Good evening, nephew."

A tall, thin figure sat on the bench in the center of the garden, several soldiers standing at attention behind him.

Uncle Amis.

Why would Uncle Amis be here of all places? No one could pass through the magical tunnel unless they had the blood of the Simmins.

Uncle Amis didn't stand. "Welcome to the ball," he said placidly.

"I need to speak with Thomis."

"He needs to attend the duties of the kingdom, and I think it best if you do not interfere."

Marc looked at the soldiers behind his uncle, not recognizing them. His uncle had brought them from D'argent. No doubt these men had served his uncle for years and would not listen to Marc, a fallen and disgraced monarch.

Marc had practiced sword fighting all his life, and while his hand wavered above his hilt, he hated to fight soldiers of Terram. "Uncle, the rebels -"

He stopped. How could he tell his uncle that his own wife could be the leader of the rebels?

"The rebels will be taken care of." His uncle finished with frightening finality in his tone.

Marc remembered what Thomis had said about the extra soldiers on the wall, and he feared for Arianna. Was she part of the rebel force? Would she try to fly over the wall?

"There will be bloodshed," Marc began.

"We will not attack first, but if they draw first – we have everything lined up."

"Just as you did thirteen years ago." Marc guessed.

Uncle Amis looked away. "No. It was not so simple as you think, Marc."

"Right and wrong is simple. Complexity comes with trying to make paths around them."

Uncle Amis' eyes flashed back. "Fifity-three D'argentians died the night of the fire, and how many of ours starved under their hard taxes?"

Hundreds.

"Dare you blame us?" Uncle Amis continued. "You were handed a kingdom bursting with resources because of the sacrifices of your father and I."

Marc shook his head. This argument was a distraction. There were more pressing problems tonight. "I need to speak with Thomis about the contract. It may be a trap."

"You arranged the contract yourself, and now you think it is a trap?"

His uncle nodded to his guards and all but two of them stepped alongside Marc in perfect formation.

Uncle Amis turned to the remaining two. "Do as I instructed you if anyone comes through the door."

No one could come through the door Marc knew.

But the guard closest to Uncle Amis was nodding dutifully until something raced by him, and he suddenly jumped back with a non-soldier like shriek.

Smiles. The gelada had come through with Marc two minutes earlier. It was nice to see that Uncle Amis' guards were so observant. If Marc had known what fools they were, he'd have sent the creature through first and snuck in himself.

Marc watched the gelada dart around the garden,

excited to find new kinds of plants to eat while his uncle's muscular guards watched the gelada like kitchen maids might watch a mouse hoping it won't dart under their skirts.

Uncle Amis ignored the creature, turning to Marc.

"Come." He commanded, and Marc was pushed forward by four guards who were suddenly very eager to leave the garden.

Marc walked, scanning ahead desperately. Any second, he'd see one of his own people, and they'd sound the alarm. But he was wrong. This back section of the garden was empty, and soon they were climbing the back stairs

Where were Marc's men?

On the wall. He realized.

Uncle Amis led up a back flight of stairs and then up a side stair.

Too late, Marc realized where they were. They were going to the upper room.

He started back down the stairs, but the guards grabbed him, dragging him.

His uncle's face was emotionless as Marc was yanked toward the room of Thrush treasure – to be locked away.

"Uncle," he gasped, struggling, "the contract is a trap!"

As he said it, he knew it with all his heart.

"Of course, the contract is a trap." His uncle replied. "That's why Thomis *must* sign it."

And then the guards yanked Marc through the open door, and Marc hit the stone floor hard.

Springing up, Marc lunged toward the closing door, but as he threw himself through, he was hit by the heavy wooden door panels and was thrown back unto the floor as the lock bolted into place.

He was alone with his useless treasure.

"Let me out! Stop!" he screamed, but he knew no one could hear him. Uncle Amis had betrayed him, and now Thomis would follow the destruction that Marc had led their kingdom to.

He searched the room for anything to help him escape. There were plenty of jewel-studded swords, but what good where they? The lock was on the outside, and he himself had tested the room. The floors and walls were made of solid limestone rocks as thick as his arm, and the roof had been made with heavy beams.

He was a prisoner as his kingdom careened toward ruin.

Trembling, he sat in the only seat in the room, the ruby-crested, dust-covered Thrush throne.

He laughed until tears were rolling down his cheeks. He'd wanted to sit on this exact throne, the savior of his people. Now he sat here, the destroyer of his people whose pride had brokered a deal with their enemies.

There was no hope!

Deep in the darkest part of the woods, Arianna landed and slid to her knees, too worn to stand.

Marc was likely heading to the castle and so was Casimir.

Would either survive the night?

And it was her fault. She could have stopped it – if she hadn't freed Casimir or if she'd told Marc everything –

But why hadn't she?

The empty forest reverberated in judgmental silence as she thought of the last words Marc had said to her.

"You couldn't love me! You loved hating me too much."

It wasn't fair that he'd said that. She *did* love him.

But yes. She hated him too. Spoiled, irrational, frustrating Marc.

The wall inside her bled black, oozing puss, and

for the first time, Arianna saw what was really trapped inside her.

Envy

How long had she wanted what Marc had? He had the power, riches and especially the hearts of his people. Even in her father's greatest hour he'd never had his people's hearts. Of that, she was sure.

She'd wanted the peaceful joy and warmth inside Marc too even though she had at times hated that as well.

She crouched on the forest floor, wishing she could touch her husband and feel his love, drawing her into the warmth she constantly starved for.

Yes. She loved this Simmins, this former king of Terram, but he was right. She couldn't truly love. She'd hated too long to know how to love.

But now, for the first time, she didn't want to hate anymore.

But how could she be free of hate?

Who could help her?

She could hear Marc's voice in her head; he would say the One Father could help her.

She winced and looked up, staring at the stars above the trees, imagining Him like her own father constantly pushing her to not dishonor the Thrush name, never fully satisfied, and judging her beneath thick brows, always slightly lowered.

But three months with Marc gave Arianna the thread of hope she needed to believe that maybe the One Father was different.

Maybe – despite all – he might have a care for her.

Trembling, she reached her hand toward the stars, imagining Him looking down at her.

"Please," she whispered.

The hate pulled back enough for her to breathe, and a familiar warmth began to combat the icy deadness.

The warmth is His love! She realized.

The constant, joyful warmth she'd felt in Marc had been the One Father's love the whole time.

Had He been drawing her, loving her through Marc, showing her what it felt like to be free?

His love felt like bathing in light, and as she stood basking in it, all she wanted was to be in it, and the hate that she'd felt and that had controlled her separated from her until she was looking down at it.

It was putrid, and she didn't want to have anything to do with it any longer. All she wanted was the love because all she wanted was Him.

"I'm so sorry!" she said softly, cleansing tears slipped silently down her cheeks carrying away the pain and anger.

Slowly, the world around her lightened. The

stars were brighter above, and suddenly, she could see the soft moonlight playing over silvery tree trunks that moments before had been black and ominous.

But the more she felt of the love, the more she knew she was not yet fully free.

The wall inside was not yet broken. She was still a slave.

Instinctively, she knew what she needed to do and armed now with a hope of Him, she was ready to leave the outstanding debt of the many who had sinned against her in His hands.

Taking a deep breath, she faced the silver-lined trees and imagined her enemies.

She could see the people of Terram, going about their daily lives, not caring that their armies had destroyed their neighbors.

She could see Marc, cocky, stubborn, and infuriatingly optimistic.

And finally, she could see Marc's father, strong at first, and then she saw him as he'd been at the end of his life, worn down by the war and decrepit with the burdens of the sins he'd caused. Strange that she'd never noticed his pain before because it was so obvious.

She spoke clearly and with all her heart. "I forgive you."

Air rushed into her as something rushed out of her.

The wall inside exploded and pain and joy filled every fiber of her being as she took the first deep, full breath she thought she'd taken since her childhood.

"I'm free!"

She looked around in her mind, almost expecting to see the courtroom at Terram's brown castle and the relieved faces of all the Terram nobility that she'd so long hoped to make bow.

Of course, they were not there. They neither knew nor cared about her years of hate toward them. The only one her hate had tortured was herself.

But now she was free, and the love grew in her until it filled every part of her, and she thought she would burst.

A movement to Arianna's left caught her gaze, and Arianna started.

There stood the mysterious woman from her childhood.

"You!" Arianna breathed

She'd wondered at times if she'd dreamed their encounter, and now she peered closely at the woman.

As a child, Arianna had thought her young — for she was beautiful in a youthful, life-giving way — but it was a deeper kind of beauty that could only come from many years of living in light and giving light.

The beauty emanated from inside her, hovering around the woman as if goodness itself had been part of her for -

Centuries. Arianna thought.

It was true, the long blond hair was actually white and only pure kindness emanated from clear blue eyes.

Arianna knew she'd never set eyes on someone so beautiful - or so old -

Except-

She remembered the man who had tempted her to use the protection spell as a wall.

The woman stepped forward. "You held me out. I tried to get back to you, but you'd taken the protection spell I put inside you and turned it into something dreadful.

"Protection spell?"

"Aye, it was only meant to protect you from the Simmin's ability to read emotion and control with it. You were in great danger for several years."

Arianna lowered her head. "I was trying to bury my pain so it – wouldn't control me."

Laelyn nodded. "By holding it in, you gave it a place to fester and grow, but you broke it."

"Love broke it." Arianna whispered. *Marc's love.*

No, not Marc's love. It had been a greater Love which was now healing her and replacing the hate.

Why had she held out love so long? She remembered why.

"There was man. He said I could use it that way; he showed me how."

"My cousin, Leonardo." Laelynn's face was sad. "He tempted you to grasp at a power you didn't understand. He took what was good and twisted it into a weapon."

Arianna didn't think it had been a weapon though she was relieved it was gone.

"I do want to thank you for the gift though. It was a good gift. It protected me many times," she said.

Laelynn looked grave. "With every good gift and every power comes the temptation to use it for ill."

"I – I didn't hurt anyone with it." Arianna defended weakly.

Laelynn laid her hand on Arianna's face like a grandma might a crying infant. "Oh child, you did. You hurt yourself for years."

It was true.

The wall had become a physical form of her bitterness, and it had been devouring her for so long that she'd stopped noticing.

Behind the wall, she'd filled a well of poison, storing all her bitterness and hate. She thought she was protecting herself, but instead, she'd destroyed herself from the inside out, poisoning herself slowly while wishing her enemies would die from the poison.

The sobs started deep within, and as Laelynn gently hugged her, Arianna allowed herself to feel the pain that she'd resisted for over a decade.

She knew it would be alright now though. She didn't need to fear the pain. She needed to feel it so she could let the pain go, and she could finally heal.

"It hurts so much," she sobbed.

Laelynn spoke softly. "It makes you the perfect leader for your people. You know their pain; you know their hearts and can lead them."

"I – I love my people, and Marc loves his people. How can we have peace?"

"And that is why you two are meant to be together, working side-by-side for the good of both. That is why a thousand years ago, you two were destined to unite your two kingdoms in peace and prosperity."

"But we aren't the heads of our kingdoms. The crown has been lost."

Arianna's mind raced. "And tonight, there's a contract, and I fear that it will bring ruin to both kingdoms!"

"Then go and warn them."

"I – I need to get into the castle."

"You shall." The lady drew back and pulled out a

thick bundle. "Years ago, I gave you a commoner's dress so you could escape your enemies. Now, I give you a queen's dress so you can face them."

Arianna took the package. It had thick paper wrapped around something soft. "But – how can I get into the castle?"

Arianna remembered the night the lady had turned the wall to fabric.

"You could get me in," she gasped.

But Laelynn was shaking her head. "I cannot this time. You must always face your own battles. My job is only to equip you and point you in the way."

"But – the guards won't let me through the gate, and there is a passage, but it will only open for the Simmins."

The lady smiled. "And that, my dear, is indeed the way. 'Tis true it will not open for you. It only opens for the blood of the Simmins, but it will open for your children."

"Except, I need it to open *now*!"

Nevertheless, the lady was fading before Arianna's eyes, and Arianna would have again wondered if she was a dream, but that Arianna stood with the bundle over her arm.

She tore it open quickly, and gasped in shock. Even in the pitch-black woods, a thousand diamonds sparkled down the bodice of the black silk dress coupled with black slippers of the same silk.

Shaking slightly, she slipped the dress over herself, letting her rough brown dress fall to the ground, forgotten.

She had not had anything so splendid since she was eight, and she turned slowly in the moonlight, letting the soft silk sway around her legs.

But her hair? She could not arrive with it in its normal knot at the back of her head.

Slowly, she pulled it out, letting it fall in soft waves down her back and only leaving the top up.

"I am the queen of my people." She whispered. "And tonight, I fight not with a sword but with the power of – hope."

Swinging her dark cape around her, she rose into the night.

Hope. So little, but so much.

Arianna flew faster than she ever had.

She had to get to the castle, and as dangerous as it was, she'd fly right over the wall, hoping that the watchmen would miss her as before.

Maybe her dark cloak would be enough –

Since almost everyone was at the palace, the town was empty as she passed it.

The stone church sat pale grey in the evening light, and the cemetery skimmed beneath her.

If only –

Arianna paused, hovering in her flight above the silent plots.

Laelynn was wrong. The passage wouldn't work.

But wasn't it worth a minute to try?

No. She decided. Every second could cost a life –

Yet, why had Laelynn said it was the way?

Cautiously, Arianna descended.

The door sat cold and dead, darkened by shadows and silhouetted by the glowing sun behind it.

Her feet crunched on dead leaves as she landed before it.

"I'm a fool!" She whispered. If her groundless hope cost her too much time, she'd be too late!

Still, she reached forth a trembling hand, but her fingers never brushed the stone.

With a crack, every ornately carved line on the ancient door glowed red, piercing the cool evening air.

How? Why? It shouldn't be working.

She checked around her. Could it be a trap?

But nothing moved in the darkening cemetery

How was this possible?

Certes, another had passed before her. Of course. Marc must have passed just before her. Somehow the magic still lingered.

That had to be it, and there was no time to consider. She needed to get into the castle!

CHAPTER 15

*S*he flew with all her might through the tunnel and minutes later, stepped into the garden, expecting to be alone, but she was not.

A tall, thin man sat on the bench, flanked by several soldiers.

"Princess Arianna Thrush," he said calmly.

Marc had told him? She eyed the soldiers. "How do you know who I am?"

"By the fact Marc married you." He lifted his lips in something that would have been a smile if it had been warm, and then he stood. His clothing was rich, and he'd have been handsome for his age if he were not so skinny.

Suddenly, she remembered him.

"Duke Amis Simmins, killer of my people," Arianna said quietly, remembering the night he'd taken Marc – so they could attack her family.

His eyes flashed. "We were not the ones who planned to attack. Your people were."

Despite the ridiculousness of his accusation, his face contorted with anger. He believed what he said.

Arianna shook her head. "I was there. I saw your men attack!"

"You were there?" He scoffed. "You were a child, scurried away to be waited on. You were not really there. I was there in the meeting halls, speaking to your father and his council. Do you think we could not read their plans. Do you think we could not feel their hate stirring under their skin?"

She stepped forward, wishing that her voice did not tremble. "What reason would they have had to attack you? The kingdom of Terram was no threat to my father."

"The union," he snapped, sneering as if the word tasted bad.

Union?

Arianna could not think what he meant. Her father would never have planned a union between the two kingdoms. She remembered how he'd always talked about Terram as small and pathetic.

"The union between you and Marc." Amis Simmins gestured.

A union was spoken of between her and Marc?

"Your connection was prophesied fifteen generations before your birth, and still your arrogant sire would not submit to it. He would not admit that he answered to any authority above himself."

Never had it dawned on Arianna that anyone but herself knew of the soul connection. She had wondered if it was the answer to the prophecy, but others had known she and Marc had it?

"We knew from your birth. There was an oracle. Both royal councils knew. It was even why we visited D'argent, hoping that your marriage would bring our starving people hope and lift the taxes that your sire suffocated them with."

She stared at him, wishing he lied...knowing he did not. They'd all known. Marc's father, Duke Amis Simmins - and her father. He had known that she had been born connected to Marc and that the kingdoms were to come together in peace and prosperity.

The shock hit her physically, and she dropped to her knees in the soft moss.

Her father had not wanted his great kingdom to bend in order for the kingdom of Terram to rise, and he'd even been willing for her to lose her soulmate to protect his power.

But more than that, she realized something else, and it was the worst of all.

She had continued in the pride of the Thrush!

She had carried the same arrogance onward, unknowingly, following her father's path into loneliness and hate, inflicting the generational curse on herself by being consumed with the same pride.

Amis Simmins was scowling. "He thought he was powerful enough to outmaneuver the prophecy."

She remembered back to the night, seeing it with a new eyes. "But, I saw the nets. Your men surrounded and attacked us."

"The nets came from fisherman's boats. The castle was along the wharf. We acted desperately and quickly when we realized what they planned for us."

She didn't want to believe it, but she could not deny it because she knew the lasciviousness and cruelty of her father and his kinsman.

And now, she found herself at another ball and on the precipice of another attack.

She opened her mouth to tell him of the trap, but she didn't trust him.

"I need to see my husband." She demanded.

"Very well. Take her to him."

He waved his hand dismissively, and the guards surrounded her, making her feel like a prisoner. She pressed back her panic because of course, she was no prisoner. Marc was a guest, and she was being escorted to her husband.

The guards walked her quickly into the donjon, but they did not pause in the great hall where she heard the crowds gathering. They led her upstairs and then up again, and up again.

They passed where she expected the family chambers to be, pushing her up another flight of stairs, down a hall, and then to a heavy door at the very end.

She knew instantly what room they were taking her to. Why would Marc be there?

Yet, she needed to speak to him so she followed willingly until one guard pulled a key out and was quickly unlocking the door. Arianna stepped back. This did not look right.

But then the door swung open, and she froze at the sight. Marc was sitting on her father's throne, its spiked back reaching up ominously, and the massive rubies glittering in the semi-dark.

She stopped, dumbfounded at seeing sweet and kind Marc on that throne of cruelty and pride, but as she stared, the second guard shoved her hard from behind and sent her flying into the room as the heavy door slammed shut.

Rolling quickly, she sat up, hearing the lock click behind her and staring about. The room was packed floor to ceiling with treasures, and at the center was Marc, still sitting on the throne.

Why had he brought her here?

Was this all so that she could not fly away again? She surveyed the room.

It was clever to bring her here. She could not fly away and would have to face him.

She looked up at him, but for once, her talkative husband wasn't speaking.

But what was there to say?

She'd lied to him, plotted against him, and worked for the downfall of his family.

How could he forgive her?

And if he rejected her, she'd feel everything.

Her bitterness had shielded her before. Bound in the murky depths of her lukewarm swamp, she'd felt protected.

But now, she was free. She'd broken the film-covered covered surface into the fresh, cool air, shivering in the bright sun - and fully exposed, naked and vulnerable, finally capable of joy, and finally capable of heartbreak.

He could destroy her.

Marc was speechless with relief that Arianna was

alright but also confused.

Why had she not flown away from the guards?

It took him several seconds to persuade himself she was really there, and then he quickly knelt beside her to help her, but she jumped up before he could touch her.

He stood slowly, facing her but still unable to see her face as the hood of her old black cloak cast shadows over her delicate features.

"Casimir is coming with his men tonight," she blurted.

"I know. I mean — I guessed."

She took another step back, her words coming out in a torrent. "I – I tried to stop him - though I should have tried long ago. You — should know I was part of plotting against your family — and you — for years! And now, he's here somewhere with his men. The attack is tonight!"

He nodded. Nothing she said was a surprise.

"And," she finished. "You shouldn't forgive me, but I am sorry."

Not forgive?

He strode over to her, grabbing her and jerking her into a hug.

"Do not ever say that I will not forgive you, Arianna." He said into her hair.

"You shouldn't – because there's more."

He doubted it, but then with trembling fingers, she took his hand, and he jolted.

"I can feel you – " He gasped.

"I know," she whispered, and while her voice trembled with unshed tears, her feelings were those of warmth with only tremors of fear - so different than the week before. Her hate was gone.

"No, I mean I can feel your feelings, Arianna. It is my family's gift."

"I know." She repeated louder. "We share powers when we touch, Marc."

He tried to think what she meant. "You could feel my feelings?" He demanded, already realizing the answer.

Her hooded head nodded in the darkness.

Marc had felt others' feelings his entire life, but the last three months had been raw. He'd poured out in hope while at times struggling with despair and rage. He'd thought he'd hidden it all, but she'd known, feeling his sorrows while watching him calmly and at times even goading him on.

"I'm sorry," she whispered, "but you must know how you helped me. It had been so long since I'd known what it felt like to be happy or – or have faith – or love."

He felt the trembling of fear grow in her, making her blood pump faster, but she pushed past it. "I love you, Marc. I didn't think I ever could love, but the hate that trapped me is gone, and now I can love you and I do –"

"You are forgiven, Arianna."

He felt a blip of shock break through her pain and flicker into anger.

"You should not forgive me. I've plotted against you, Marc. Even now, it's beyond what I can fix." Her voice trembled. "Do not give so large a gift – to forgive."

"Because you are too proud to accept it?" He asked as he held her tight. "You think I don't understand the need to be forgiven? I thought you dead. I blamed myself, and Petir taught me that the One Father had already forgiven me. I had to accept the forgiveness, and when I did, I was free – to love and live again."

The pain was swirling in her, and Marc began to doubt, but he strengthened himself against her despair, resisting the suffocating darkness of it and filling his lungs in a deep breath, and as he did, he prayed truth.

You are loved, cherished, forgiven.

"There will be a war. I – there is much evil –" Arianna murmured.

"Then we face it, but not by holding hate against each other. Take the forgiveness, Arianna. Then, we will face the world."

She buried her head, and he was drawn back into the whirlwind with her, the battle silent but the hardest he'd ever fought.

Accept the love, His love, and mine. He begged, his heart whispering into hers.

And then, the whirlwind dissipated, and the anger and pain settled, and she gave a long sigh.

"Thank you for forgiving me."

"I already had. Nothing changed – except that you *finally* accepted it. Besides," he teased, holding her tighter, "you've proven how miserable unforgiveness can be."

She laughed, a real, full, beautiful laugh like when they'd been young, and he relished the sound of it as he cupped both sides of her face to turn it up toward himself.

He stared: The beautiful, laughing golden eyes were back!

"Your eyes. They have light again."

He stood and felt her. The scars of the brokenness were still there, but consuming the pain was something that surrounded the pain, overriding, recoloring it and making it beautiful.

As he pulled her in, he felt her soul bursting, overflowing with one guiding light that ruled every other part of her - hope.

The seeds of hope had worked; the entire time, they'd been growing roots under the surface.

Not an ounce of pain had been wasted. Every tear had been multiplied for good.

Crossing the room, he rifled through a trunk until he found the object he was looking for: the D'argentian crown. Covered in 120 diamonds, it sparkled in the semi-dark. Plucking it up, he walked to his wife.

Even in her old black cape, she was and would always be his queen, and reverently he placed the crown on her head and gave a low bow.

Her large gold eyes sparkled with unshed tears, and her face showed such promise, he expected her to reach up to kiss him.

Instead, she stepped back lifting trembling fingers to the tie on her cape. It fell off, and Marc stared at the dress worth at least as much as two tanneries, and her bodice sparkled with diamonds as she dropped into a graceful curtsy before him.

"Where did you get that?" He peered at the dress.

She beamed. "It is from a lady who I think is my fairy godmother."

"Laelynn?" Marc guessed. "Have you ever asked her why she gave you a tannery instead of a mill or a bakery or something that did not stink?"

Arianna laughed, feeling it bubble out of all the joy that was already taking root and bearing fruit inside her.

"There is your laugh again," Marc breathed. "How I've missed it."

He drew her into a kiss. They were still prisoners, but they had never felt so free, and they were still tanners, but they had never felt more like royalty.

Sounds and yells broke through from outside, and Arianna straightened.

"It's starting, Marc. How do we get out of this room?"

"We are locked in," he said slowly.

"You are also a captive?" She gasped.

He looked up at the ceiling "Aye, but I have an idea. We will use the power of the air."

"I'm not that powerful!"

"But together we could be! Do you remember when we were children and combined our powers and flew?"

Arianna remembered it well because it had been so frightening. They'd been out of control and in great danger, shooting past the roof of her father's enormous palace.

Marc took both her hands. "We are stronger together."

She blinked at him. They were more dangerous together – to themselves and others.

He shook his head. "Do you believe we are meant to be together, Arianna?"

"Yes." She did. There was no doubt. They were destined to be united.

"And," his voice slowed. "Do you believe we were we brought together for this moment?"

She paused. How could they not have been?

Hesitantly, she slipped one hand out of his and reached into the air, but as she did, she determined to trust.

It wasn't giving into the air. The air was not in control.

It was a trusting of the One who made the air. It was worship, and she was not alone in her worship. She was united with Marc in the worship, and together they were standing back and recognizing the air for what it was, one of His many displays of power and goodness to his children.

Arianna felt like she understood the air for the first time in her life, but more than that, she understood herself for the first time as well. In the center of the hope of the One Who had made everything, she saw her gifts and callings clearly, all perfectly used for His good purposes. For in light of His love from which everything proceeded, everything finally made sense.

He was what she'd been missing, and now, finally recognizing it, she saw the rest of the world in the correct order for now that she trusted the Maker, she could see it all clearly.

She didn't have to fight. She could just rest in Him.

And on that thought, she slowly pressed out, effortlessly exerting power many times what she thought possible. She watched the throne rise, its spiked back shooting toward the ceiling.

From out in the courtyard, Casimir listened intently.

He was kneeling inside the fake frosted wooden cake, but things were not going as planned.

The schedule had been changed.

The cake was supposed to have been drawn into

the center of the party at the beginning, long before the signing of the contract.

Why had it not been brought in?

Now, he feared it would be too late to stop the contract from being signed.

The unsuspecting baker sat patiently out in the courtyard, the party in the garden just over the inner wall, with no idea that his cake was a ruse, a wooden box frosted and decorated exactly like the one the baker had made switched out by his passionate and D'argent-sympathizing son.

Casimir weighed his choices. If he broke out of the cake now, it would alert the guards, but if he didn't, he could miss the signing of the contract.

The contract could not be signed; it would doom them all.

The music over the wall halted long before it was scheduled to pause, and he knew he needed to act immediately.

Unlatching the top of the wooden cake, he jumped past the surprised baker, racing up to the garden gate.

A single guard was at the gate, and he started to reach for his sword, but Casimir, trained in the circus for over a decade, used the man's shoulder as guide and flipped over the man's head before twisting and wrapping his arms around the man's neck from behind.

It was a large guard, but for years Casimir had been stronger than even a large man, and he squeezed hard, finally feeling the man give in to unconsciousness.

Dragging the man around the gate, he deposited him in the hedge before swinging the gate fully open.

Two more unconscious guards, some quiet threats to the frightened baker, and four minutes later, 40 more of Casimir's followers, all dressed as guests, were edging around the courtyard.

Now, Casimir jumped up to the seat of the wagon. Driving the cake deep into the heart of the garden, he passed over a dozen guards, but none noticed him beside the colossal cake.

The cart creaked as it was pulled into the center of the party-goers, and Casimir scanned the scene, narrowing in on King Thomis Simmins who was just finishing signing his name in dark red ink.

Instantly, colors burst out of the document, and the words shifted, changing the contract before the shocked onlooker's eyes.

"You have signed your people away to be slaves of Ecoptia and the Jade Isles!" The ambassador's voice boomed.

King Thomis Simmins stared, his nostrils flaring slightly, but his voice was surprisingly calm. "How is it that the words on the contract can change?" He demanded. "How does the blood of a dead animal do such a thing?"

The ambassador grinned. "It does if the dragon is not dead. Dragons are master deceivers, and they care for their own."

"You mean you are in league with a dragon?" The king asked steadily.

"He is our ally."

"No dragons can be an ally of humans. They are tricksters, serpents – right from the very beginning, these monstrous serpents have sown lies!" Thomis Simmins declared.

The ambassador grinned. "And yet, he has made you and your people our slaves by his cunning."

The king shook his head vehemently. "'Tis you who are slaves. All who fall to the lies of the serpents will be their slaves."

The ambassador grabbed the glowing contract, reading it aloud. "From henceforth, the kingdoms of the Simmins will be enslaved to the people of Ecoptia."

Thomis Simmins raised the contract above his head and started to speak, but he was drowned out by cries that were breaking out through the crowd.

Casimir knew this was his moment.

They'd been betrayed as he knew they'd be.

Casimir jumped onto the center of the table, raising his hands above his head.

"Once again, the Simmins betray the Kingdom of D'argent!" He hollered.

With a quick sweeping glance, Casimir could tell who his countrymen were.

Their faces matched his own heart — anger and a resolve to fight. Tonight, was the night to break free from the Simmins rule, but they had to fight now – here in the heart of the Simmin's castle. They had to take the castle tonight!

Casimir had every eye on him, and he knew what to do. He'd always been good at leadership, and now he rallied the lords of D'argent to himself. "Pick up your arms, brothers! Our children will not be slaves to the people of the Jade Isles – to their dragon! Seize the traitorous Simmins and their foolish king!"

The murmurs of the guests were growing; in a minute Casimir would have a mob, but just as the chaos was about to unleash, a large, muscular man stepped smoothly between him and the king.

Petir, the physician, looked calmly at Casimir. "Stop! You are calling for blood."

He did not raise his voice, but it was clear, his gaze unbending. His steely composure calmed the crowd instantly, and the murmuring stopped.

The garden had gone completely silent, and every

eye was on Casimir and Petir, and Casimir knew he'd have to fight the man to prove his strength and his worth, but of every man in Terram, Casimir hated to fight this one. He knew of the good this man had done on the coast.

"Stand aside," Casimir said, looking past him to Thomis Simmins who still held the contract.

But the large man jumped up on the table, never taking his eyes from Cassimer. "Stand down, friend. There are many innocent lives here."

"What life is the life of slavery?" Casimir interrupted. "Let me die fighting for freedom."

The physician shook his head. "Do not call for fighting. There may be another way – "

Casimir needed the nobles of D'argent to fight, and this fool was calming them. Reaching out his palms, he focused on the fountain, grasping one large wave in his mind and then – slapping it into the physician and knocking him back off the table.

"Tis the magic of Thrush!" someone gasped.

The physician staggered to his feet. "No. This is older." He shouted. "I've seen this; it is older than Thrush."

Older. The physician knew more of Casimir's origin than Casimir did.

"Stand aside," Casimir ground again. "I know you

helped the needy in the D'argent kingdom. I've no desire to kill you.

Guards were stepping forward. He cared not for them – but because of the women and children in the garden, he'd have to be careful.

Casimir measured the bowls of fire, looking past them to the pool. It was dangerous. He could carry the bowls on waves and take out the ambassadors of the Jade Isles, but he feared harming the onlookers.

He knew his men were surrounding the place. At his signal, they'd close in, but if only there were not children here! It made everything tricky.

"Brothers! Countrymen! This is an hour we must come together!" The physician was on the table again. "Divided we are vulnerable, but united—"

Casimir shot more water at the man, but this time, the man had his sword up, slicing the hard surface of the water and breaking it before it could slap him down.

Casimir tried again, but the physician ducked and rolled, and when Casimir pummeled him with a second wave, he evaded it.

Enough. His people were in place. There would be casualties, but if they won tonight, all of D'argent would be free.

Casimir raised his hand to give the signal when

something huge crashed into the center of the table, throwing food and splintered wood everywhere.

In the shocked silence, Casimir drew toward the broken gold and ruby pieces and stared.

It was a huge, broken throne, large enough to seat three men.

The Thrush throne.

"Look!" someone yelled. Gasps sounded all around Casimir, and slowly he raised his eyes.

There, hovering above all, was their long-lost queen.

She looked barely human.

She was the D'argientian flag itself with diamonds sparkling across her front and with a crown, the Thrush crown, on her head.

But the most shocking thing was that she did not fly alone. There beside her, his hand clasped in hers, flew Marc Simmins.

A *Simmins* was flying.

How—?

The prophecy was *real*.

To Casimir's left and then his right the D'argentian lords were lowering their swords, recognizing Arianna as the rightful heir to their throne, but Casimir felt his own men's eyes on him. Here was their queen. Would they reject her, or embrace the uniting she brought with the Simmins?

The physician stared across at Casimir, his broad mouth tight. Slowly, he lowered his sword.

Casimir looked to Aria, *Queen Arianna.* His queen.

She stared at him, her face commanding though her eyes pleading as a long-time friend.

Casimir knew what he must do. A decade had led to this moment, and he was the one who had to do it.

If he bowed in peace, all resistance would be subside.

He lowered his sword, and without turning, he knew his men did the same.

Slowly, he bowed at the waist and around him, his men, the last of the D'argentians, and all the people of Terram did the same.

They were united.

CHAPTER 16

*A*rianna followed Marc and landed beside Thomis.

With a flourish, Marc drew his sword and stood before the ambassadors of the Jade Isles.

"We want no more dealings with you. You take your hideous contract and leave our land. We stand together against your wicked ways."

The ambassador chuckled, and his deep baritone laugh echoed through the garden.

"Your king has signed your people away to the king of the Jade Isles."

He held up the contract.

Blood – dark and yet iridescent in the firelight.

Arianna had never seen dragon's blood, but she'd

heard of it. If the king signed as representative of his people, he and his land would be devoured in the fire of the dragon if they went back on the contract.

How had Thomis agreed to such a thing?

Trickery, she realized. This was why there had been so much yelling. This was the hidden power and curse of the Jade Isles. They served a dragon!

The ambassador's white teeth glimmered, and he stood so close to Marc that spittle hit Marc's face as he spoke. "This changes nothing. The king's signature is binding. The people ruled by the Simmins are slaves of our dragon, bound to do his bidding."

Marc didn't move. "Slaves of trickery? Do you realize *what* you serve? It may make slaves of us, but it preys on your souls – and your heritage. You know the legends of the dragon. They want your most precious. It may give you power. It may even enslave your enemies – but at what cost? Your chil-"

"Enough!" The ambassador snapped. "The contract is signed. You've united your kingdoms – but for what? Through the strength of the dragon, we have the power destroy you and your lands."

Marc searched for a way to change what had happened. There was nothing. In his arrogance, he'd joined the kingdoms only to doom them to slavery.

The entire time, the greatest threat had been the Jade Isle ambassadors. They'd stoked Marc's pride, promised a peace they never wanted, and used sorcery of the darkest kind – with a dragon — to trick them all, and the treaty Marc had set in motion was a trap, and Thomis had fallen into it.

Now, how many would suffer because of Marc's conceit?

How many were doomed?

He looked to Thomis, expecting his brother to look pig-like with flared nostrils, but his brother was smiling.

As Marc stared, Thomis held up the contract, the scarlet red ink glowing in the candlelight.

"Then it is a good thing that this contract does not bear the king's signature." Thomis said.

"It bears *your* signature." The ambassador snapped.

"Aye." Thomis agreed.

"And you are the king."

"Nay. I am not."

"You lie!" the ambassador bellowed.

Thomis walked over to one of the flaming bowls, holding the paper above the flickering tongues. "If I were the king, this contact would be indestructible, correct?"

"Of course," the ambassador growled.

He looked at Marc, his smile widening, pleased with his brilliant move. "And I am not, since the true king was married two minutes *before* midnight.

Thomis tossed the contract into one of the bowls of fire, and the flame turned scarlet red as it burned the paper to ash.

With a flare, Thomis took off the Simmins crown, holding it high.

"It's been a ruse the entire time. I foresaw this deception, knowing the ways of the dragon that controls your people. Upon my uncle's counsel, I led you into exposing yourself to everyone."

He crossed to Marc and handed the crown to the priest who held the crown high for several seconds.

Dumbfounded with shock, Marc knelt, and the priest placed the crown back on Marc's head.

Marc had been crowned similarly two years earlier, but he knew he was a different man. Before he'd felt worthy. This time he knew he was not, but he also knew he was called.

He'd not take his calling lightly. Slowly, he turned and faced his beaming people and then turned back to the Ecoptian ambassadors of the Jade Isles.

The head ambassador was sweating. "There will be a war between our two peoples."

Marc stepped forward. "This was no treaty. This was betrayal, and now you have shown yourselves to be the enemy that you are. The kingdoms of D'argent, and Terram will be united against you."

Marc motioned, and Uncle Amis stepped forward, his thin lips forming a big smile as his little group of soldiers surrounded the furious ambassadors and corralled them toward the outer gate.

The evening that Casimir had planned for retribution had become a night of unification.

Now, Casimir stood quietly, watching Arianna through the crowd.

She was a beautiful queen, and she looked like an angel beside her handsome king husband.

"The queen has taken her rightful place."

Casimir turned and started.

The pale-haired woman beside him was familiar though he knew he'd never met her before.

The woman was looking past him to Arianna. "She is where she should be."

The woman's words hurt because the woman was right, and because for the first time he fully realized the truth. He'd loved Arianna, and he'd been a fool to love her.

The lady read his thoughts, and her voice gentled. "A queen has also been chosen for you."

The words were absurd, and the lady's wise eyes twinkled when he stared at her and asked. "A queen for a penniless minstrel?"

"A queen for the future king of a great kingdom."

She had to be wrong, but her gaze was clear. This woman did not lie.

"Who are you?" he asked.

"My name is Laelynn. You know that you are not of the house of Thrush."

"Yes."

"You were raised by nobility within the Thrush capital, but you were found abandoned on the beach as a baby and thought to be of noble blood because of your powers."

"Yes," he whispered. No one had known that except the D'argentian parents who had adopted him, and they had died the night the palace burned thirteen years earlier.

The woman continued. "Your kingdom is a place of great power and magic – but also of great danger, and before you can claim your kingdom, you must prove your worth."

A thousand clues pointed to the truth of her words, but still, he dared not believe them.

She had turned back to watch the ball, looking warmly at Arianna, like a mother may look at a child she is especially proud. "Her quest is complete; yours is about to begin."

"And where is my quest?" he demanded.

She smiled softly. "You already know."

He did. Where else could it be?

The Jade Isles.

It had been thirteen years since Arianna had heard D'argentian music, and she listened to the pipes of her homeland, lilting and playful like the sea, and then from across the garden, a lone Terramite drum began to thump in time to the melody. Its steady beat added strength and honesty to the trilling song of the sea. Moments later, more drums joined as well as a few lutes, strumming out honest chords, harmonizing with the D'argentian melody.

The instruments complimented each other perfectly, and the age-old songs were richer than they'd ever been. Harmony filled the garden, and Terramites and D'argentians began to pair up and to dance together.

The dancers swirled before them, and Arianna wished Marc would dance with her. It was time to be whisked away into happiness.

Instead, her king husband stood between her and Thomis watching the dancers with satisfaction.

"You were right about the contract brother," Marc said.

Thomis smirked. "I am *always* right, brother."

Marc smirked too. "However, the party was my idea. I told you it would be a good party and bring peace, did I not?" He bumped Thomis with his elbow.

Thomis scowled. "Oh come now! 'Twas I who saved the kingdom!"

"Well, yes, after you *stole* the kingdom."

"*Borrowed* it — in order to save it."

Marc laughed. "Well, I think I have the perfect idea to thank you for my months of being a tanner."

Thomis straightened. "And what would that be, *brother?*"

"I'll send you as an ambassador over to the kingdom of Vasilocha."

Thomis sniffed. "Ambassador? But ambassadors like people and persuade them of things."

"Aye, and we know you have no persuasive skills at all." Marc rolled his eyes in a clearly un-kingly way.

"I would never use my powers for small things." Thomis gasped. "Only in times of great distress."

Marc laughed. "And while you are being an ambassador, you can ask the king of Vasilocha to pay for half the road you want between our kingdoms so we can establish trade."

Thomis struggled several seconds before sighing. "Very well."

Marc wasn't done teasing. "You may even meet a princess."

"I doubt it."

Thomis turned to Arianna. "I had thought Casimir was the Thrush, but it was you. I am relieved you were not shot coming into the castle tonight for I had so many extra guards posted on the wall! It's a miracle you made it over!"

Marc snapped to attention. "Over the wall, Arianna? That was dangerous."

She placed her hands on her hips. "I did not go over the wall tonight! Your magical door — that you *claim* only opens for the blood of the Simmins — opened for me! 'Tis obvious that it is not so strong a magic as you thought!"

She was pleased to see Marc's jaw drop.

"It opened for you?" He took a step forward.

She giggled. "Well, it lit up, and I walked through it."

Thomis did not look surprised. Instead, he shot Marc a smile. "Congratulations, brother."

Marc did not take his eyes from her. "Wife, do you realize what this means?"

Wife. She liked that word on his lips. It was far past time for them to kiss – and dance.

"The magic door is broken?" she asked distractedly.

Marc laughed, sliding his hand over her waist. "It means you have the blood of the house of Simmins in you."

How? She was a Simmins now, and strangely she felt only joy at that – but how could she have their blood?

Suddenly, she understood what he meant.

"A child," she whispered, stunned.

Marc gave her one of his most endearingly mischievous grins. "*Children.* Remember, in my family we have twins."

Arianna laughed. "Twins. Of course."

Two babies gifted.

Two kingdoms united.

Marc finally leaned forward, kissing her firmly, and as his hands closed over hers, they climbed the air in dance together until they were far above the crowd, and they were surrounded by nothing but stars.

They were no longer alone – but right where they should be – together.

Two nations joined together in hope.

A LETTER FROM THE AUTHOR

hank you so much for reading Arianna and Marc's story!

Years ago, I prayed for an opportunity to do something to fight sex trafficking and was grateful to be part of this collaboration.

As a mother of an adopted child, I thought through how healing from childhood trauma works as I wrote this book, often speaking truths to myself.

God works. God does miracles, and God heals.

His love is powerful and will grow beauty out of the pain as He grows our faith and opens our eyes to understand His love.

On the last pages of this book are ways to fight human traffiicking and a list of other books in the Hope Ever After series.

I hope you join me again!

There is more to some of these characters' stories.

Petir settles down – until he finds an ethereally beautiful woman almost dead in the woods.

(Of course, **Domini** is not a normal woman. She is the queen of the Heizebels, daughters of the goddess who strive for their own power. Moments before she can take her throne, she is betrayed and is now hunted by dragons.) She is confused by Petir and his people. How can these people of weakness have such strength from their One Father?

Sign up for my newsletter at veritysandahl.com/ newsletter, **and I'll send you a free two-page epilogue for Marc and Arianna as well as Petir and Domini's free novella in the next couple months!**

You can also follow me on Instagram where you'll find a lot of posts about writing, things God is teaching me, and many pictures of my umpteen (awesome) kids. My Instagram account is @veritysandahl

Thomis is going to go on his ambassador trip, but more important than the road he hopes to build, he will find a princess. Is it possible for such a logical, mastermind to find love? He clearly needs a sunshiny opposite to turn his carefully-calculated world upside down! If you'd like to read a book about Thomis, let me know, and I'll prioritize writing it! My email is veritysandahl@gmail.com

Laelynn's cousin **Leonardo** gets into way more mischief in Daleena Taylor's book "A Faithful Hope." He's up to his old tricks and having a wonderful time causing lots of trouble!

And finally, **Casimir** is much more than a noble. He will be the hero in a myth retelling I'll have coming out August 15th, 2025 that is part of another incredible charity collaboration. He will learn of his parentage and past as he travels to the Jade Isles, but more than that, he must save an incredible princess only to discover that he needs her – and the faith that sustains her – to be saved himself and to find that he's barely begun to realize the legacy he's meant to leave. (And **Brion** and **Smiles** will be along for the ride!)

I was grateful to return to the **King Thrushbeard** fairytale. Four years ago, as the world crumbled, my father passed away, and I heard the King Thrushbeard tale for the first time.

I deeply resonated with the princess trying to hold on to her faith, and as I wrote the story, I wrestled with God over hard questions, finding Him sufficient again and again to answer my questions.

The book, **Power of the Pawn,** was so close to my heart that I was hesitant to share it with the world, but I'll be publishing it November 9th 2024, and I will be looking for ARC readers!

If you are interested in being an ARC reader, email me at veritysandahl@gmail.com.

POWER OF THE PAWN

ARC READERS NEEDED SEPTEMBER
2024

*I*s God in control when the world has gone mad?

Weeks after father's death. Lady Avelina is forced into marriage with a common miller, a man who murdered her father's knights and aided her traitorous stepbrother. When the king, the church, and her guardian betray her, Lina must determine if it was they or God who lowered her station.

And how is her hedge-born husband so well educated? What is he hiding from her?

Sir Fredric, the second son of the earl of Kensington, laid down his sword two years prior, desiring peace with God and man, but when his friend offers him a chance to protect the Lady Avelina by marriage, he agrees, knowing he will soon need to pick up his sword again.

Can he persuade Lina to love him despite her belief that he is a lowly miller?

And when he discovers their enemies are allied, can he protect those he loves before his wicked brother, the future earl, discovers the true terms of his marriage?

HOW YOU CAN SUPPORT O.U.R.

The purpose of the "Hope Ever After" series is to spread hope and be an avenue to support and raise awareness in the fight against human trafficking and slavery. Here are some facts about human trafficking:

Every 30 seconds another person becomes a trafficking victim.

There are 40.3 million modern-day slaves estimated by the International Labour Organization. 1 in 4 slavery victims are children. 71% of slavery victims are women and girls.

Trafficking in persons is now the 2nd largest illicit industry in the U.S., 2nd only to the drug trade. It is also the fastest growing form of international crime. (UNICEF)

It is estimated that the human trafficking enterprise generates roughly $150 billion dollars a year.

The O.U.R. has aided in the arrest of over 4,000 predators, recovered over 6,000 survivors, and supported over 1,000 operations.

HOW CAN YOU HELP?

Educate yourself on how to recognize a victim of trafficking.

Take a stand against pornography, which leads the demand for sex trafficking.

Pray. Pray for victims and pray for those in the operations who are searching and rescuing victims.

Buy all the books in the "Hope Ever After" series! All the proceeds from this series go to the O.U.R. to fight and end sex trafficking.

WE HOPE our books inspire you to join the fight against human trafficking because God's children are not for sale. Thank you so much for your support!

"The only thing necessary for the triumph of evil is for good people to do nothing." -Edmund Burke

"There are three types of people: those who fight, those who help the fighter, and those who do nothing." -Dennis Prager

HOPE EVER AFTER SERIES

"Hope Ever After" is a collection of twenty hopeful and uplifting fairy tale retellings. Each book is written by a different author so it can be enjoyed in any order. The proceeds from this series are donated to the O.U.R. (Operation Underground Rescue) to rescue children from sexual exploitation and trafficking. Be sure to collect all twenty, as the entire series, put together, forms a rainbow, a symbol of hope and of God's love!

An Ambitious Hope: A Red Riding Hood Retelling by Lucy Winton

A Gentle Hope: A Beauty and the Beast Retelling by Sarah Carlisle

287

A Silent Hope: A Wounded Lion Retelling by Madisyn Carlin

A Fairest Hope: A Snow White Retelling by S. Lee Poole

A Crowned Hope: A Prince and the Pauper Retelling by Kayla Eshbaugh

A Golden Hope: A Rumpelstiltskin Retelling by Chelsey Noelle

A Beautiful Hope: An Ugly Duckling Retelling by Leialoha Humpherys

A Renewed Hope: A Princess and the Pea Retelling by Robyn Sarty, Scarlett Luna Strange, and Selina De Luca

A Charming Hope: A Frog Prince Retelling by Ashley Evercott

An Enduring Hope: A Wild Swans Retelling by Jes Drew

A Cascading Hope: A Little Mermaid Retelling by Yakira Goldsberry

A Midnight Hope: A Cinderella Retelling by Stefanie Lozinski

A Faithful Hope: A Blue Bird Retelling by DaLeena Taylor

A Gracious Hope: A Sleeping Beauty Retelling by Robyn Sarty

A Wishful Hope: An Aladdin Retelling by Sarah Beran

A Healing Hope: A Rapunzel Retelling by Selina De Luca

A Wingless Hope: A Thumbelina Retelling by Sydney Winward

A Secret Hope: A Goose Girl Retelling by Scarlett Luna Strange

A Frigid Hope: A Snow Queen Retelling by Amanda Thompson

A Last Hope: A King Thrushbeard Retelling by Verity Sandahl

www.ingramcontent.com/pod-product-compliance
Lightning Source LLC
Chambersburg PA
CBHW052027240626
47153CB00006B/1980